TEARS OF DESTINY

P.CIBI SARAVANA

Contents

1. "Threads Of Fate" — 1

2. "The Whispers Of Fate" — 4

3. "The Masked Spirit The Unveiling" — 7

4. "The Shadow And The Frost" — 10

5. "The Play Of Fate" — 12

6. "The Echo Of Silence" — 14

7. "A World Of Silence" — 16

8. "A Spark Of Light & The Arrow Of Hope" — 19

9. "The Whispers Of Rebellion" — 23

10. "A Shadow Of Betrayal" — 26

11. "A Cross Road" — 30

12. "Whispers In The Night" — 33

13. "Echoes Of Fate" — 37

14. "The Legacy Of Pain" — 40

15. "The Seeds Of Friendship" — 45

16. "A Dance Of Fate" — 49

17. "Echoes Of Strength" — 53

18. "The Rose Of Revelation" — 59

19. "A Shadow Of Threat" — 62

20. "A Shadow Falls" — 69

21. "Together Whispers" — 73

22. "The Archer's Fury" — 76

23. "The Archer's Return" — 81

24. "A Spark Ignites" — 88

25. "The Shadow's Game" — 91

26. "A Father's Shadow" — 94

Contents

27. "A Dance Of Shadows"   97

28. "The Locket's Promise"   106

29. "The Price Of A Lie"   111

30. "A Birthday Revelation"   118

31. "The Match Of Fury "   122

32. "The Bridge Of Fate"   130

33. "A Bridge Of Light"   134

34. "The Game Of Shadows"   136

35. "The Weight Of Truth"   146

36. " The Masks Of Fate"   153

37. "The Crown Of Ashes"   156

38. "The Serpent's Shadow"   160

39. "The Serpent's Dance"   166

40. "The Shadow's Dance"   171

41. "The Night Of Revelry"   176

42. "A Dance Of Blades And Broken Hearts"   180

43. "New Beginnings"   189

44. "Coronation"   193

45. "The Tapestry Of Fate"   196

46. "A New Life"   199

47. "Echoes Of The Past"   202

48. "The Reunion"   204

49. "The Return"   207

50. "The Cosmic Realm"   210

CHAPTER ONE

"THREADS OF FATE"

In the intricately woven fabric of our contemporary global landscape, Hanjojio emerges as a singular urban tapestry, meticulously crafted to reflect the multifaceted cultural currents of our time.

This metropolis, a synthesis of South Korean tenacity, Japanese elegance, Chinese tradition, and Indian vibrancy, bears a name chosen with deliberate intent. 'Han' symbolizes the indomitable spirit of South Korea, 'Jo' evokes the refined grace of Japan, 'Ji' embodies the enduring heritage of China, and 'O' resonates with the kaleidoscopic hues of India. Though an invention of fiction, Hanjojio serves as a mirror to the bustling reality of our interconnected world. Its streets teem with the vitality of diverse cultures converging and thriving, offering a vivid portrayal of unity amid diversity. Join me on a journey through the labyrinthine alleyways of Hanjojio, where the delineations between imagination and reality dissolve into an enchanting mosaic of human experience.

In 21ˢᵗ Century,

The city, a cacophony of neon and rain, seemed to devour V(28) whole. His white shirt, once pristine, was now a crimson canvas, mirroring the blood staining his hand as he clutched his chest. Each breath was a ragged rasp, a desperate plea for air that seemed to slip further away with every passing second.

He lifted his head, his vision blurred by the relentless rain. His eyes, wide and frantic,searched the swirling chaos for a flicker of hope, a glimmer of salvation in the neon-drenched abyss.

A figure emerged from the shadows, a silhouette against the blinding glow of the street lamps. Ria(28). Her face was ashen, her eyes reflecting a desperate hope battling the rising panic within her. She sprinted towards him, her footfalls barely audible against the thunderous downpour.

V, his legs failing him, crumpled onto the rain-slicked asphalt. Ria caught him just before he hit the ground, his weight pulling her down with him. Under the flickering streetlight, she cradled his face, her trembling fingers searching for a flicker of life in his rain-lashed features.

A truck horn blared, shattering the rhythmic symphony of the rain. Headlights erupted, blindingly bright, filling the narrow street with an unwelcome brilliance. The truck, a behemoth of metal, barreled towards them, out of control. Without a moment's hesitation, Ria threw herself over V, her body a desperate shield against the impending impact.

Metal screamed against asphalt. A deafening crunch echoed through the night. V and Ria were flung through the air, their bodies rag dolls in the blinding headlights. Then, silence. The truck, a mangled wreck, rested against a lamppost. The driver stumbled out, dazed, a silhouette against the fading headlights.

On the rain-slicked pavement, V and Ria lay sprawled, separated by a chasm of twisted metal. Their eyes met, locked in a silent exchange, a desperate plea for connection amidst the encroaching darkness.

V's eyes flickered open, fighting against the relentless rain. His hand reached out, fingers grasping weakly, a desperate attempt to bridge the chasm that now separated them. Ria, battered but defiant, saw the movement. She dragged herself towards him, leaving a trail of blood on the slick asphalt.

Their eyes met, and her hand, mirroring his, reached out. Their fingers trembled, stretching across the impossible distance between them. A single tear escaped V's eye, tracing a path through the rain on his cheek.With a final surge of strength, she inched closer, her hand almost touching his. Their eyes locked, a desperate plea for connection in the face of encroaching darkness. The light faded from Ria's eyes, reflecting the emptiness that consumed V.

The rain continued to fall, washing away the tears and the blood, leaving only the stillness of death.

A voice, ancient and echoing, resonated through the stillness.

"Every life, a thread in fate's tapestry. But what happens when those threads are broken?"

CHAPTER TWO

"The Whispers of Fate"

Aripple of cosmic energy distorted reality, twisting the scene into a vortex of light and darkness. "Let's rewind... and unveil their story."

But this was not a scene from the mortal world. This was the Book of Fate, a swirling vortex of cosmic knowledge, and the Assistant, a being of pure light and energy, hovered before it, his form shimmering with a distress he couldn't contain.

Two glowing threads, once intertwined, now lay severed, a testament to his error. He frantically flipped through the pages, his luminous fingers trembling, searching for a solution. He pressed his hand against the page, desperate to mend the broken threads, but the damage was irreversible.

"My mistake... Their fates... broken," he whispered, the words echoing through the vast expanse of the Cosmic Realm. A wave of panic washed over him. His usually harmonious glow turned chaotic, casting distorted shadows across the Book of Fate.

The Assistant recoiled, his body shrinking in on itself, a visual embodiment of guilt. He knew he had to act.

He raced towards the Elder God, a swirling vortex of cosmic energy, a being whose very presence defied comprehension. The Elder God's eyes, galaxies swirling within their depths, opened, their gaze piercing the Assistant's very essence.

"Guilt burdens you," the Elder God's voice boomed, resonating through the very fabric of reality.

The Assistant bowed low, his form trembling. "But our laws forbid interfering with mortal lives! How can we help them?"

The Elder God's gaze held a hint of amusement. "Every failure has a solution."

"But... spirits? They are unpredictable!" The Assistant's voice was laced with fear, a stark contrast to the Elder God's calm assurance.

"Trust is irrelevant. Offer them freedom, and they'll accept. Keep them separate. Their ignorance is essential," the Elder God declared, his voice echoing with a power that sent chills down the Assistant's spine.

The Elder God faded, leaving behind a vision of V and Ria, their paths diverging, a stark reminder of the fractured destinies.

The Cosmic Realm fractured, reality warping and twisting, shards of reality solidifying into a breathtaking glacial landscape. The Assistant, his form shimmering with apprehension, stood before this newly formed world.

The Assistant stared at the fractured landscape, the cold air biting at his ethereal form. He had to trust the Elder God's plan, however reckless it seemed.

The weight of his mistake, the burden of their shattered fates, pressed heavily upon him. But how could he, in good conscience, allow these spirits, these unwitting pawns, to bear the burden of mending a broken destiny?

The Assistant's heart ached for V and Ria. He had witnessed their connection, their love for each other, so strong it even resonated within the Book of Fate. He could not bear to see those threads unravel.

"I will guide them," he whispered, his voice laced with determination, "But I will do so with compassion, with hope."

His form shimmered, his gaze fixed on the swirling nebulae above, a reminder of the vastness of the cosmos and the delicate balance of fate. He knew that the path ahead would be fraught with peril, but he would not falter. He had to trust the Elder God's plan, however perilous it might be.

The fate of V and Ria now rested in the hands of those he could not control, those who sought their own freedom, unaware of the pivotal role they would play in the delicate dance of fate.

CHAPTER THREE

"The Masked Spirit the Unveiling"

The Assistant, his form shimmering with a mixture of apprehension and hope, stood before the Cosmic Snow Temple. It was a majestic structure carved from celestial ice, its spires reaching towards the swirling nebulae that painted the vast canvas of the cosmos. Before him, a vortex of cosmic energy raged, a gateway to the ethereal realm where spirits resided.

The Assistant extended a hand towards the vortex, his touch drawing a surge of energy from its core. The air crackled, the swirling vortex pulsed, and a figure materialized, shrouded in darkness. This was the Masked Spirit, a being whose masked face absorbed light, his true form hidden from mortal eyes.

"Spirit," the Assistant spoke, his voice resonating with a strange urgency, "a mission. Succeed, and you'll be free of that curse. Protect a mortal named Ria. Guide her from the darkness."

The Masked Spirit's masked face, a void of shadow, flickered as if trying to absorb even the Assistant's words. He spoke, his voice raspy, echoing with the weight of his forgotten dreams. "Freedom... a forgotten dream. Who is this, Ria? Why your concern?"

The Assistant, his heart heavy with the burden of their shared fate, projected a vision into the Masked Spirit's mind. First, a vision of Ria as a child, her innocent face, a mirror of purity and joy. Then, the vision shifted, showing Ria as she had become, her face hardened, her eyes reflecting the darkness that had consumed her. Finally, the Assistant showed a vision of Ria, triumphant, her eyes filled with the light of hope, her spirit unbroken.

"You'll learn as you progress," the Assistant said, his voice filled with a desperate hope. "Many fates depend on your victory."

The Masked Spirit's mask flickered, a hint of determination momentarily piercing the darkness. "Very well."

He plunged back into the vortex, disappearing into the swirling chaos. The Assistant watched, his gaze fixed on the fading image of the Masked Spirit, a mix of hope and apprehension in his heart.

He could only pray that the Masked Spirit, guided by the promise of freedom, would fulfill his part in the grand plan. The Assistant knew that this was just the beginning, the first step in a perilous journey. The fate of V and Ria, and the delicate balance of the cosmos, now hung precariously in the hands of this masked spirit, driven by a forgotten dream of freedom and a promise of redemption.

The Elder God stood upon the summit of the Cosmic Snow Mountain, a majestic figure of swirling energy and celestial light. The wind howled, whipping through the icy peaks, yet the Elder God remained unmoved, his presence a beacon of power amidst the frozen landscape. Below, the world stretched out in a breathtaking vista of snow-capped mountains, their peaks disappearing into the swirling nebulae that painted the cosmic sky.

From the swirling mists, the Elder God summoned the Masked Female Spirit. She appeared before him, her masked face revealing nothing, a stark contrast to the swirling galaxies that reflected in the Elder God's eyes.

"Spirit," the Elder God began, his voice resonating with power and a hint of anticipation, "I—"

The Masked Female Spirit, her voice sharp and impatient, cut him off. "Get to the point. I have no time for games."

The Elder God's eyes narrowed, his gaze piercing the Masked Female Spirit's impenetrable mask. He knew her kind, their pride, their hunger for freedom, the bitterness that fueled their existence.

"Guide a mortal named V," the Elder God said, his voice calm and unwavering, "Help him, and you'll be free of your curse."

The Masked Female Spirit smirked, a cold, sardonic expression that did little to ease the Assistant's apprehension. "Freedom. Fine, but expect no gratitude."

The Elder God, his gaze unwavering, projected a vision into her mind. He showed V as a child, his face etched with the scars of a troubled past, his eyes reflecting the pain of abandonment and fear. The Masked Female Spirit's expression hardened, a flicker of empathy momentarily piercing the ice in her eyes.

"I'll do it," she said, her voice now laced with a steely determination. "For my freedom."

She vanished, dissolving back into the swirling mists. The Assistant, his form shimmering with a mix of anxiety and relief, materialized beside the Elder God.

"My task is done," he said, his voice hushed, his words heavy with a sense of accomplishment and a hint of unspoken worry.

The Elder God smiled, a knowing smile that seemed to hold secrets that spanned the breadth of creation itself. "Good. Let the games begin."

The Elder God's gaze swept across the Cosmic Snow Mountain, his eyes gleaming with a knowing anticipation. The Assistant felt a shiver run down his spine, a cold premonition of the unseen forces now set in motion. The fate of V and Ria, once intertwined, now lay in the hands of two spirits, bound by their own desires, unaware of the grand plan that orchestrated their every move. The Assistant could only hope that their ignorance would be their salvation. The grand game had begun, and the Assistant could only watch as the pieces moved on a cosmic chessboard, their destinies intertwined in a delicate, dangerous dance.

CHAPTER FOUR

"The Shadow and the Frost"

The Cosmic Snow Temple stood tall and silent, a beacon of celestial ice against the backdrop of swirling nebulae. The moonlight painted the snow-covered courtyard in an eerie glow, reflecting off the towering spires of the temple. The Male Spirit, shrouded in darkness, stood in the heart of the courtyard, his masked face a void that absorbed even the moonlight.

His gaze was fixed on a distant point in the cosmos, a fragile blue sphere hanging in the vast expanse. Earth. It was the home of Ria, the mortal he had been tasked to protect, the reason he had chosen to embark on this perilous journey.

"Ria... How can I, shrouded in darkness, lead her toward the light?" he whispered, a hint of warmth in his raspy voice, a warmth that surprised even him. The warmth wasn't just for Ria, but for the forgotten dream of freedom that flickered within him.

He clenched his fist, determination hardening his features. "I will learn," he whispered again, "For her sake... and perhaps my own."

Meanwhile, on the summit of a distant snow-capped mountain peak, the Masked Female Spirit paced restlessly, leaving scorched imprints in the pristine snow. Each step was a violent eruption of icy energy, a stark contrast to the serenity of the celestial landscape. She halted, her gaze fixed on Earth, a world she viewed with disdain and indifference.

"Breaking free from this curse... that's all that matters," she muttered, her voice laced with bitterness. "V... he's just a means to an end."

She summoned a blast of icy energy, shattering an ice formation, a testament to her power and her volatile nature. "I have my own goals," she growled, her voice echoing with a chilling determination. "This mission better be worth my time."

The Assistant, watching from the confines of the Cosmic Snow Temple, knew that the two spirits, now separated, were heading towards an unknown fate. The paths they would tread, guided by the whispers of the Elder God, would be fraught with danger and uncertainty. The fate of V and Ria, their fragile connection, now rested in the hands of these two enigmatic beings, each driven by their own motives, each harboring a secret desire for freedom. He could only hope that their journeys would lead them not to destruction, but to redemption.

CHAPTER FIVE

"The Play of Fate"

The Elder God and the Assistant stood before a shimmering vision, a celestial tapestry woven from stardust and whispers of fate. It depicted the Masked Spirit and the Masked Female Spirit, their forms now separated, their journeys leading them towards their destined paths.

The Assistant watched, his gaze filled with apprehension. The spirits, driven by their own desires, were headed towards an unknown future, their every move dictated by the whispers of the Elder God, a being whose true motives remained shrouded in mystery.

"Great One," the Assistant said, his voice laced with doubt, "their fates are so fragile. Is this the right path? What trials await them?"

The Elder God smiled, a unsettling smile that seemed to hold a chilling secret, a secret that echoed the vastness of the cosmos and the intricate dance of fate. "They will face their ultimate adversary: Fate itself." His voice boomed, reverberating through the very fabric of the Cosmic Realm.

The Assistant, his heart pounding in his chest, felt a chill run down his spine. He knew that the Elder God's words held a profound truth, a truth that resonated with the very core of their existence. Their destinies had been disrupted, the intricate tapestry of fate unraveling. And now, the spirits, tasked with mending the broken threads, would face a formidable challenge - a clash of wills, a battle against the very force that shaped their existence.

"Their destinies have been disrupted," the Elder God continued, his voice echoing with an ominous tone. "It's a battle of wills."

The Assistant stared at the shimmering vision, his anxieties mounting. He understood the Elder God's words, the weight of their meaning. The spirits, in their quest for freedom, would encounter unforeseen obstacles, their paths fraught with peril. They would face trials that could either break them or forge them into something new, something extraordinary.

The Elder God's smile widened, a hint of mischief dancing in his eyes. "Let us witness the clash," he said, his voice filled with a curious anticipation, "Fate against their indomitable spirits."

The Assistant, his heart heavy with apprehension, could only watch as the spirits embarked on their perilous journeys. The Elder God's true motives remained a mystery, a shadowy enigma within the vast expanse of the cosmos. The Assistant could only pray that these spirits, guided by their desire for freedom, would find their way back to the light, their destinies interwoven once more in the grand tapestry of fate.

CHAPTER SIX

"The Echo of Silence"

The sterile white walls of the hospital room seemed to amplify the silence. Ria's father cradled his newborn daughter, his calloused hands gentle as he whispered her name, a prayer for a life that had just begun. Her mother, her face glowing with the exhaustion and joy of new motherhood, watched with bated breath. But baby Ria didn't cry. A tense silence fell over the room, a silence that held the weight of unspoken fears.

"Doctor," Ria's father asked, his voice laced with worry, "What's wrong?"

The doctor, his face etched with regret, approached them, his gaze meeting theirs. "I'm sorry," he said, his voice soft, "Your daughter is deaf and mute."

Ria's mother stifled a sob, clutching the sheets, her body shaking with a grief that seemed to consume her. Her husband, his eyes glistening with unshed tears, gently placed a hand on her shoulder, his touch a silent promise of comfort and support. He looked at his daughter, his expression filled with a fierce love that transcended words.

"She's beautiful," he said, his voice unwavering, "She'll make this world listen."

Years passed, a blur of milestones and memories. Ria, now four years old, sat between her parents, her small hand guided by her mother's. Her mother traced the signs in the air, teaching her the language of silence, the language of her heart. The sign for "mother" was a simple gesture, yet it resonated with a profound love and understanding. Ria's face lit up with a triumphant smile, her eyes sparkling with a joy that spoke volumes.

The city lights blurred past the car windows, a symphony of neon and noise. Ria, bundled in a warm coat, bounced in her seat, her eyes wide with excitement. Her parents were taking her out for a birthday dinner, a celebration of her resilience, her spirit that shone brighter than any city light. She signed "car" and "go," her eyes sparkling with anticipation.

The phone rang, shattering the quiet joy of their family ride. Ria's father answered, his voice strained.

"Get to the office, now!" The Head Manager's voice crackled through the speaker, laced with anger.

"I'm with my family," Ria's father replied, his voice firm, "I'll be there in the morning."

"Family dinner? That's your priority?" the Head Manager scoffed, his voice dripping with contempt.

Ria's father gripped the steering wheel, his knuckles white, about to retort, when blinding headlights filled the car. A truck's horn blared, a deafening sound that ripped through the silence of their journey. Ria's mother screamed, instinctively clutching her daughter, her body trembling with fear.

The car swerved, fishtailing on the wet road. It careened off the asphalt, rolling and tumbling before coming to a violent stop.

The wail of sirens echoed through the night. Ria, her small body limp, was loaded onto a stretcher by paramedics, her eyes closed, the world fading to a blur of colors and sounds she couldn't hear. The ambulance sped away, sirens wailing, a desperate race against time, carrying with it a small child and the weight of a shattered life.

CHAPTER SEVEN

"A WORLD OF SILENCE"

The hospital room, a sterile white box, felt suffocating. Ria woke, a wave of confusion and pain washing over her. Her bandaged hand, a symbol of her broken world, was immobile. Panic tightened its grip, a silent scream trapped in her throat.

She tried to sign for her parents, but her hand hung lifeless, a stark reminder of her loss. Her eyes, filled with a desperate hope, met her uncle's. His face, contorted with grief, reflected the tragedy she had experienced. He shook his head, tears brimming in his eyes, a silent confirmation of the unspoken truth. Her parents were gone.

The doctor entered, his expression solemn, his words heavy with sorrow. "I'm sorry... your parents didn't survive."

Ria's heart shattered. The world, once filled with the love of her parents, had suddenly become an abyss of silence.

"I will adopt Ria," her uncle declared, his voice firm despite the pain etched on his face. "I'll take care of her." He signed the adoption papers, his hand steady, a testament to his unwavering love and resolve.

Ria and her uncle walked out of the hospital, hand-in-hand. The world, once vibrant and full of sound, now felt tinged with loss. The laughter of children, the hum of the city, all seemed muted, drowned out by the echo of her parents' absence. But a glimmer of hope shone in her uncle's eyes, a promise that she would be loved, that she would not be alone.

Their new home was a place of both comfort and sorrow. Ria sat in the living room, surrounded by the remnants of her parents' lives - their photographs, their books, their favorite music. Her aunt, a picture of forced cheerfulness, moved around, unpacking boxes, her smile strained, her movements tense. The front door slammed shut, shattering the uneasy peace. As her aunt turned, her smile vanished, her gaze meeting Ria's. A flicker of resentment, barely concealed, crossed her face.

In the kitchen, a mop was thrown at Ria's feet. "Clean this whole house," her aunt barked, her voice cold and sharp, "And make sure it's spotless." Ria's small hand, still bandaged, appeared tiny around the mop's handle. Her aunt's gaze was cold, her cruelty evident in her eyes.

Later, at the dinner table, Ria picked at a plate of cold food, her appetite gone. Her aunt, across from her, enjoyed a steaming meal, her gaze cold and dismissive.

That night, in her room, Ria clutched a photo of her parents, tears falling on their smiling faces. She opened a jewelry box, each trinket a painful reminder of lost love. Her parents' love, once a beacon of light, now felt like a distant memory, a fleeting dream.

Days turned into weeks, weeks into months. Ria tried to tell her uncle about her aunt's mistreatment, but her aunt always intercepted, her grip tight on Ria's arm, silencing her with a look. She could see the anger and frustration simmering in her uncle's eyes, but he never intervened.

One night, Ria eavesdropped at her aunt's door, her heart pounding in her chest.

"She's a burden," her aunt whispered into the phone, her voice laced with malice, "I'll get rid of her as soon as I can."

Ria retreated to her bed, trembling, clutching a teddy bear, the world closing in around her.

Weeks later, her uncle, his eyes filled with concern, signed to her. "Ria, it's time for school again."

A flicker of hope, a faint spark, lit up Ria's sad eyes. School, with its echoes of laughter and learning, was a place where she could find solace, a place where she could escape the darkness that had consumed her life. She reached out, her hand finding his.

The world was filled with silence, but within Ria's heart, a silent hope, a whisper of resilience, flickered on. She knew that her life, though marred by tragedy, would continue, and she would find her way, guided by the memories of her parents, their love her guiding light, their whispers a beacon in the darkness.

"A Spark of Light & The Arrow of Hope"

The school cafeteria was a cacophony of noise, a swirling vortex of voices and laughter that washed over Ria like a chaotic wave. She sat alone at a table, her heart heavy with a loneliness that seemed to echo the silence of her world. She unfolded a crumpled paper airplane, a crude drawing of a girl with crossed-out ears. It was a cruel reminder of the taunts and whispers she had endured, a symbol of the world's lack of understanding. Tears stung her eyes, a silent plea for acceptance, for a place where she could belong.

Later, in the school hallway, Ria walked with her head down, her books clutched to her chest, a shield against the world's indifference. She bumped into someone, her books scattering across the floor like fallen leaves. A hand reached down, helping her gather them. Ria looked up, meeting Aira's kind eyes.

"Hi, I'm Aira," Aira said, her voice warm and welcoming. "What's your name?"

Ria hesitated, then signed her name: "Ria." She gestured towards her ears, then shook her head, a silent explanation of her disability.

Aira's eyes widened, a flicker of understanding illuminating her face. She signed, "It's okay. We can be friends."

Ria smiled, a genuine smile, for the first time in a long time. A spark of hope, a glimmer of light, pierced the darkness that had enveloped her.

A montage unfolded, capturing the blossoming friendship between Ria and Aira over the years. Uplifting music set the tone, accentuating the joy and comfort they found in each other's presence.

Schoolyard: Aira and Ria strolled side by side, sharing secrets and laughter. Aira signed animatedly, her hands a whirlwind of movement, while Ria listened intently, her face alive with amusement.

Classroom: Both girls excelled academically, assisting each other with assignments and celebrating their achievements together. They confidently raised their hands, actively participating in class discussions, their voices a chorus of understanding.

Aira's Home: Aira fed Ria with care, a tender gesture of love. Ria gazed at Aira with adoration and gratitude, finding in her a maternal figure she craved, a warmth that filled the void left by her parents.

Park: Aira pushed Ria on a swing, their laughter ringing through the air as they raced through the park, their carefree laughter a testament to the joy they shared.

Aira's Room: Aira and Ria sprawled on the floor, surrounded by a sea of books and drawings. Their laughter filled the room, mingling with animated gestures as they shared dreams and aspirations. Aira's brother, entering quietly, observed their interaction, a friendly smile gracing his lips. He caught Aira's eye, she acknowledging him with a subtle nod. His gaze lingered on Ria, a spark of curiosity and interest flickering within his eyes. Without a word, he slipped out of the room, leaving the girls immersed in their conversation, unaware of the brief, silent encounter.

School Library: Aira guided Ria in learning sign language, expanding her vocabulary and communication skills, opening a world of possibilities.

The montage ended, leaving the viewer with a sense of hope and warmth. The friendship between Ria and Aira was a testament to the power of understanding, the beauty of acceptance, the resilience of the human spirit. They were a beacon of light in a world often shrouded in darkness, a reminder that even in silence, love and connection could blossom.

The school grounds buzzed with the energy of Sports Day. Cheers erupted from the sidelines as students competed in a whirlwind of activity. Aira, her face alight with excitement, pulled Ria(10) towards the archery event, a vibrant splash of color amidst the sea of school uniforms.

A regional champion, Abi(28), a woman radiating confidence and skill, showcased her talent. Her arrows, guided by a steady hand and unwavering focus, hit bullseye after bullseye, a testament to years of dedication and practice.

Ria, captivated by Abi's precision and grace, leaned forward, mimicking the archer's stance, her gaze glued to Abi's every move. A dream began to stir within her, a dream that transcended the silence that had defined her life.

As Abi left the archery range, Ria approached, a hesitant smile gracing her lips. She gestured towards the bow, a silent plea for a chance to try.

Abi, her eyes meeting Ria's, sensed the girl's eagerness. "You want to try?" she asked, her voice warm and encouraging. She offered a beginner's bow, a simple tool designed for novices.

Ria, her eyes fixed on Abi's professional bow, shook her head, a silent but firm refusal. She pointed to the professional bow, a gesture that spoke volumes about her determination.

"This one?" Abi asked, her eyebrows raised in surprise. "Are you sure?"

Ria nodded, her gaze unwavering, her determination shining through. Abi, sensing a spark of something extraordinary, reluctantly handed over the bow.

"Just focus on hitting the board," Abi advised, her words laced with caution.

Ria, ignoring the advice, her eyes locked on the bullseye, drew back the string. She released the arrow, a silent missile launched towards its target.

THUD. Bullseye.

Abi stared, speechless, her jaw slack with astonishment. "Have you shot before?" she asked, her voice laced with disbelief.

Ria shook her head, her eyes shining with a newfound confidence.

Abi, sensing a talent that went beyond experience, handed Ria a special arrow, her personal lucky arrow. "You have potential," she said, her voice filled with admiration. "This is my lucky arrow. Use it well. My dream is to win the world championship!"

Abi departed, leaving Ria alone with her newfound dream. She clutched the arrow, a symbol of possibility, her eyes fixed on the distant target, a tangible representation of her aspirations. A new dream, nurtured by a moment of inspiration, had taken root, a dream that promised to break the boundaries of silence and soar towards a world of possibilities.

CHAPTER NINE

"THE WHISPERS OF REBELLION"

Ria, her eyes alight with excitement, signed animatedly about the archery event, her passion evident. Her aunt, watching with a smirk, turned her attention to Ria's uncle, a flicker of something sinister passing across her face.

"Archery isn't for you, Ria," her uncle declared, his voice firm, his words laced with a subtle disapproval that cut through Ria's joy. "Focus on your studies."

Ria, her heart sinking, pleaded with him, her gestures full of hope, her determination shining through her eyes. She was not a child who could be easily silenced, a spirit that refused to be subdued. But her uncle remained unmoved, his gaze cold and unwavering.

"Enough, Ria!" he snapped, his voice sharp, his words cutting through her pleas. "Go to your room!"

Ria, her dream shattered, retreated to her room, tears streaming down her face. She clutched Abi's lucky arrow, a tangible reminder of her newfound ambition, her determination burning brighter than ever.

The night was alive with a strange stillness, the silence broken only by the ticking of the clock. Ria, unable to sleep, her heart heavy with frustration and despair, decided to escape, to find a moment of peace, a moment to breathe. She slipped out of her room, her steps silent, her movements fueled by a rebellion that had been simmering within her for far too long.

The park was a haven of shadows and moonlight. Ria, running through the park, her heart pounding in her chest, heard the barking of a dog. The dog, a large German Shepherd, lunged at her, its teeth bared, its growls echoing in the night. Ria stumbled, crashing into a boy sitting on a bench. They both tumbled to the ground, the dog lunging again.

The boy, a boy named V the same age as Ria, scrambled up, shielding Ria with his own body. They struggled, the dog's ferocious barks echoing in the night. V, surprisingly strong for his age, fought back, a fierce determination in his eyes.

Ria, grabbing a stone, threw it at the dog. The stone, a missile of defiance, hit its mark, the dog yelping in pain and retreating.

The boy, a scratch on his arm, smiled at her. "Thanks," he said, his voice barely a whisper.

Ria, her heart beating with a mixture of fear and adrenaline, smiled back.

But the moment was shattered. V's father rushed towards them, his face contorted with fury.

"Son! What are you doing out here?!" he roared, his voice echoing through the park.

Ria, her heart pounding, ducked behind the bench, her gaze fixed on the scene unfolding before her.

The father, his hand raised, slapped V across the face. "How dare you sneak out!" he shouted, his voice thick with anger. He grabbed V's arm, dragging him away, the boy's whimpers swallowed by the night.

Ria watched, her heart filled with a mixture of worry and empathy, as they disappeared into the darkness. As she turned to leave, she spotted a half-broken locket lying on the ground. She picked it up, tracing its edges, the metal cool beneath her fingertips. It was a simple locket, its design worn with time, yet it spoke of a love once cherished. A bittersweet smile touched her lips. She tucked the locket into her pocket, a silent promise to remember the brave boy she had met, a boy who had shielded her from danger, a boy who, like her, carried the weight of unspoken pain.

CHAPTER TEN

"A Shadow of Betrayal"

The classroom buzzed with pre-exam tension, a symphony of nervous whispers and rustling papers. Ria(19), her heart pounding in her chest, gathered the courage to approach the teacher's desk. She had a question, a simple question that she couldn't voice. She wrote it on a slip of paper, her fingers trembling.

Their fingers accidentally brushed as she handed him the note. Ria flinched back, her body tense, a silent scream trapped within her. The teacher, his eyes lingering on her, offered a reassuring smile, his voice a low murmur that sent a shiver down her spine.

"We'll discuss this later... privately," he said, his words laced with a subtle threat.

Ria retreated to her desk, her body trembling, her gaze darting towards the clock. The minutes stretched into an eternity, each tick of the clock a countdown to a fate she couldn't comprehend.

As the classroom emptied, the teacher slipped a folded note into Ria's hand, his eyes meeting hers, a sinister smile twisting his lips. Her fingers trembled as she read the words:

"Teacher's office. After school. Come alone. Or you will suffer."

Fear, a cold, insidious grip, tightened around her heart. She glanced at Aira, her best friend, who sensed her distress, her gaze filled with concern.

The teacher's office, a sterile space of dusty books and fading portraits, was transformed into a chamber of horror. The teacher, a mask of civility now torn away, locked the door, a sinister smile twisting his features. Ria shrank back, clutching her books, her gaze darting towards the exit.

"Just a few minutes, Ria," the teacher said, his voice a menacing whisper as he leaned closer, his gaze predatory. "Cooperate with me."

He unbuttoned his shirt, his eyes gleaming with a sinister intent. Panic surged through Ria. She stumbled back, colliding with a table. He grabbed her, hurling her to the ground. His weight trapped her, suffocating her.

"You can't escape," he hissed, his voice dripping with malice, "Women like you are just props."

Ria fought back, kicking, screaming, her body a desperate vessel of defiance. His slap echoed in the confined space, a sharp, stinging pain. Tears streamed down her face, her silent screams a testament to her terror. He leaned closer, his hand reaching for her.

BANG!

The door splintered under a relentless assault. Aira, her fury blazing in her eyes, burst through, her presence a whirlwind of righteous anger.

The teacher, scrambling for the window, shoved it open with a primal grunt. He cast a venomous glare at Ria, his eyes filled with a mixture of hatred and fear, and vanished into the night.

Aira rushed to Ria, helping her to her feet. They fled the office, the chilling memory of the teacher's threat, the fleeting glimpse of him sprinting away, the only reminder of the horror they had just endured.

Aira's house, a haven of warmth and comfort, offered a stark contrast to the raw emotions swirling in the air. Soft music played, a soothing melody that did little to calm the storm within Ria's heart. Aira, her voice gentle, cleaned Ria's wounds, the antiseptic stinging on her cuts. Ria sat in silence, her gaze lost, haunted by the evening's events.

The "For Sale" sign, swinging in the breeze, replaced the one that read "Ria's Family." Ria stood frozen, tears brimming in her eyes, her belongings scattered across the lawn like shattered dreams. Her suitcase lay open, its contents spilling like the fragments of her life. Her aunt and uncle emerged from the house, smirking, their faces a mask of indifference.

"So long, Ria," her uncle said, his voice dripping with venomous disdain. "Thanks for the property. Should've known better than to trust your own blood, eh?"

He spat on the ground near her feet, a final act of cruelty. "Your father was a fool to leave it all to you," he continued, his voice low, laced with a venomous hatred. "At least he died before I had to... take care of things myself."

Aira, her gaze steely, stepped forward, shielding Ria with her body. Her hand closed over Ria's, a silent promise of support.

"Let's go, Ria," Aira said, her voice cold, her eyes filled with a dangerous resolve.

Ria, collapsing into the seat of Aira's car, her body wracked with sobs, signed, her voice broken. "Why? What did I do to deserve this?"

Aira, tears welling up in her own eyes, held Ria's hand tight. "I'm so sorry, Ria," she signed, her voice strained. "I'll make things right. I promise."

She turned away, staring out the window. Her reflection in the glass was a mask, hiding a guilt that gnawed at her soul, a secret plan that simmered beneath the surface.

A flashback montage played out in Ria's mind:

The Teacher's venomous words: "You'll never amount to anything."

Her Uncle's cruel declaration: "He was lucky to die before I had to arrange his demise."

Her parents' faces, their voices filled with love.

Abi, the fearless archer, hitting bullseye after bullseye.

Ria, wiping away her tears, felt a new resolve harden her gaze.

"Where can I go?" she signed, her voice filled with a desperate hope. "What about my studies?"

Aira's smile was bright, reassuring... but calculated.

"Don't worry," she signed, her words laced with a promise that held a hidden agenda. "I'll take care of you."

Aira opened the door to her guest house, revealing a bright, welcoming room – a haven of sunlight and art supplies.

"This is for you, Ria," Aira said, her voice soft, her eyes filled with a deceptive warmth. "Be yourself."

Ria stepped inside, the tension draining from her shoulders. A small smile touched her lips.

"It's beautiful," she signed, her voice filled with a hesitant gratitude.

Aira's eyes gleamed with a mix of love and determination... and something Ria didn't see – manipulation.

"No more worries," Aira signed, her words laced with a chilling certainty. "We'll face the future together."

The future, Ria knew, was uncertain, but she trusted Aira, her best friend, her protector. Little did she know, that trust was about to be shattered, replaced by a web of secrets and a dangerous game of power.

～

CHAPTER ELEVEN

"A Cross Road"

Morning light flooded Ria's room, a gentle reminder that a new day had dawned.Ria(22), her sleep-filled eyes blinking open, was startled by the insistent buzzing of her phone. She grabbed it, her fingers fumbling with the screen, and saw a video message from Aira(22). Aira, her face bright, signed with a playful energy, "I'm waiting!"

Ria threw back the covers, a whirlwind of energy as she threw on clothes and raced down the stairs. Her heart pounded with a mixture of excitement and apprehension. She was ready to start a new chapter in her life, a chapter filled with promise and a hint of uncertainty.

Aira leaned against her sleek car, tapping her foot impatiently. A grin spread across her face as Ria burst out of the house, her breath catching in her throat.

"About time!" Aira signed playfully, her voice filled with a lighthearted teasing.

Ria, breathless but grinning, gestured an apology. Aira laughed, a sound that echoed the joy of their friendship, and unlocked the car. Ria slipped into the luxurious seat.

The car pulled away, the city a blur of colors and sounds. Ria glanced back at her house, a place that now held only memories, both joyful and painful. Excitement and nerves battled within her, a potent mix of anticipation and fear.

Aira caught her eye, raising an eyebrow, her gaze inquisitive. "Ready?" she signed, a hint of something unreadable flickering in her eyes.

Ria's smile was determined, her eyes resolute. She nodded firmly. The car accelerated, propelling them toward a future filled with promise... and secrets.

Meanwhile, at a bustling bus stop, V(22), a young man with a determined stride, sprinted towards a moving bus. He caught the driver's eye, a plea for mercy in his desperate gaze. The driver, sensing his urgency, slowed down. Gasping for breath, V clambered aboard, his heart pounding with a mix of relief and frustration.

He settled into a seat, catching his breath, his gaze sweeping over the passengers. The bus was stuck in traffic, a sea of impatient faces reflecting the city's relentless pace. He noticed a little girl, her face crumpled with disappointment, struggling with a deflated balloon.

"Need a hand with that?" he asked, his voice gentle, a flicker of compassion warming his eyes.

The girl nodded, handing him the balloon. V, his hands nimble and kind, inflated it, a silent act of kindness. A quote, printed on the balloon, caught his eye: "If it's meant for you, it will find its way to you."
He handed the balloon back, a smile gracing his lips. The girl, her face beaming with gratitude, planted a kiss on his cheek.

Aira, her car trapped in the same traffic jam, watched this scene unfold through the window. She smiled, a calculated smile that hinted at a hidden agenda. Suddenly, a gust of wind, a mischievous breeze, snatched the balloon from the little girl, carrying it towards Aira's car. The girl cried out, her face crumpling with disappointment.

Ria, inside the car, saw this. She swiftly opened the door, stepped out, and caught the balloon, a spontaneous act of kindness. She smiled at the little girl and handed it back.

Inside the bus, the men, distracted by Ria's sudden appearance, crowded around for a better look, trapping V in the middle. He struggled to see what was happening, his heart pounding in his chest.

Back in her car, Ria watched the little girl climb back onto the bus. She crumpled the balloon, a hardened expression passing across her face. The balloon, a symbol of fate and fortune, had been a reminder of the unpredictable twists and turns of life.

Inside the bus, V, catching a glimpse of the girl getting the balloon back, looked up through the bus window as Ria got back into her car. Their eyes met for a fleeting moment, a connection forged in the midst of chaos.

The bus pulled away, the engine a rumbling hum that seemed to echo the uncertainties of their lives.
V, tracing the outline of Ria's face on the misted window, felt a pull, a sense of connection that he couldn't explain. He sensed something in her, a strength, a resilience that resonated with his own.

Ria, staring at her reflection, her face filled with determination, watched the city blur past the window. The world was a tapestry of possibilities, a kaleidoscope of emotions, and she was ready to embrace it, to carve her own path.

They arrived at the universitas, a grand building that promised a world of knowledge and opportunity. At the same time, V stepped off the bus, his gaze fixed on the imposing structure. He was unaware of the women standing just a few feet away, their destinies intertwined in a complex web of fate, a web that was about to unravel.

CHAPTER TWELVE

"Whispers in the Night"

Thunder cracked, a deafening roar that shook the room, sending shivers down V's spine. A blinding flash of lightning illuminated the room, casting a ghostly glow on his startled features. He jolted awake, his heart pounding in his chest, the adrenaline coursing through him. The window exploded, shards of glass flying like a thousand glittering daggers.

V scrambled out of bed, his body a symphony of instinctive reactions. He gathered the glass, the shards cutting into his finger, drawing blood.

In the bathroom, he washed the cut, wincing at the pain. A flashback flickered in his mind: his mother, her face etched with concern, tenderly tending to his childhood scrapes, her warmth a stark contrast to the loneliness he felt now. He reached for a first-aid kit, a half-broken heart-shaped locket catching his eye. He smiled, remembering his encounter in the park, the memory a beacon of hope in the darkness.

Suddenly, a voice, cold and commanding, whispered in his ear.

"V, listen to me," the Female Spirit's voice whispered, a chilling sound that sent a shiver down his spine.

V spun around, his eyes wide, his heart pounding in his chest. He saw nothing.

"Turn around, you fool!" the spirit's voice echoed, a hint of irritation lacing her words.

V, his body trembling, turned slowly, his heart racing. In the mirror, a shadowy figure appeared, its face obscured by a mask, its presence undeniable. He scrambled back, his fear a tangible force, a cold dread that enveloped him.

He stood frozen in his bedroom, his eyes darting around the room, searching for the source of the voice, his mind reeling. He bumped into his desk, sending books crashing to the floor, the sound amplifying his terror. He spun around, but there was nothing there.

He tried to convince himself that it was his imagination, but the air felt heavy, oppressive, the silence punctuated by the ghostly echoes of the spirit's voice.

"Will you turn around already?" the spirit's voice commanded, a hint of annoyance lacing her words. "I'm tired of this game. Look at me!"

V, his body a vessel of trembling fear, slowly turned. The spirit stood before him, her masked face obscured, her presence an undeniable force. He blinked, struggling to comprehend what he saw. She stepped closer, her voice cold and commanding. "I am a spirit. You will cooperate.
Understand?"

Her gloved fingers, icy and ethereal, grazed his chin. He nodded hesitantly, his mind still reeling from the encounter.

"Are you really a spirit?" he asked, his voice filled with a mixture of fear and disbelief. "I mean, you're wearing a mask. Isn't that supposed to be scary?"

The spirit's eyes narrowed, her expression cold, her gaze piercing. "I am not ordinary. Be quiet."

He offered his hand, a gesture of uncertain friendship. "Let's be friends."

The spirit ignored him, her eyes filled with a chilling determination. She raised her hand, a surge of powerful energy emanating from her. V slumped onto his bed, his body succumbing to a deep sleep, the spirit's will overriding his own.

The Female Spirit circled him, her gloved fingers tracing the locket on his chest, the locket he had found in the park. The locket hummed softly under her touch, a whisper of a forgotten love, a connection to a life he never knew. A predatory glint entered her eyes, a dangerous gleam that reflected her sinister intentions.

"I will reclaim my freedom," she whispered, her voice a chilling promise, "This boy holds the key."

With a surge of energy, the spirit vanished, leaving V asleep, unaware of the forces that now played around him, the secrets that were about to be revealed.

Moonlight bathed Ria's bedroom, its ethereal glow casting long shadows across the walls. She stirred in her sleep, her dreams filled with a strange, unsettling energy.

A street market, a cacophony of sights and sounds, assailed Ria's senses. She felt trapped, the chaotic crowd a suffocating force. She closed her eyes, seeking solace in the darkness.

The scene shifted, a breathtaking garden blooming in the moonlight. Fragrant flowers, their petals unfurling in the soft glow, released a sweet fragrance that filled the air. A butterfly, its wings a kaleidoscope of colors, landed on her shoulder. It took flight, joining a swirling dance of butterflies, their wings a vibrant tapestry of beauty and grace.

From the heart of the display, the Male Spirit emerged, his face gentle, his eyes filled with a comforting warmth. Before Ria could speak, a panda cub, its fur soft and cuddly, waddled towards her, followed by its parents. A tiny elephant, playfully nudged Ria's hand, a symbol of a world filled with joy and wonder.

The scene faded, leaving behind a lingering sense of peace and tranquility.

Ria woke, her heart racing, the unsettling feeling from her dream lingering. She grabbed a glass of water, seeking solace in the familiar act of taking a sip.

A hand, its touch ethereal, reached out from the shadows, startling her. She scrambled out of bed, grabbing a knife, her eyes wide with fear.

"Ria, calm down," the Male Spirit signed and spoke softly, his voice a soothing balm to her panicked heart. "I'm a spirit, and I'm here to help."

Ria, her grip tight on the knife, didn't lower it. She swung it wildly, a desperate act of self-defense. The spirit, his movements swift and graceful, easily dodged her attacks. With a flick of his hand, he disarmed her, the knife falling to the floor with a clatter.

Ria, her fear turning to anger, grabbed a book and threw it at him. He dodged again, his movements fluid and effortless.

"It seems this isn't the right time," he muttered, his voice laced with disappointment.

He gently brushed a strand of hair from Ria's forehead, a touch that emanated a soft, calming light. Ria, her body relaxing, felt a sense of peace wash over her.

"Fear not," he smiled, his eyes filled with a comforting warmth. "I'm here to guide you. We shall talk... in due time."

A butterfly, its wings a kaleidoscope of color, landed on the spirit's hand. He smiled at Ria, then faded into the darkness, leaving behind a lingering sense of hope.

The night, once filled with terror, had been touched by a whisper of something extraordinary.

CHAPTER THIRTEEN

"Echoes of Fate"

V, struggling to navigate the labyrinth of his new life, scrolled through his phone, watching eerie Instagram reels about ghosts. The clips, a macabre blend of spooky stories and unsettling visuals, stirred unsettling memories of his encounter with the Female Spirit.

"Great. Now my phone's haunted too," he muttered, his voice laced with a mixture of amusement and apprehension.

He laughed with his classmates, trying to mask his unease, but a wave of dizziness washed over him, his eyesight blurring. He brought his hand to his face, noticing a smear of blood on his fingers. He had a nosebleed. Panic flickered in his eyes, a primal fear that he couldn't shake.

In the washroom, he leaned over the sink, trying to staunch the bleeding. The dizziness overwhelmed him, his body a vessel of weakness. He collapsed, his head pounding, his vision fading.

A burst of water from a broken pipe splashed his face. He gasped awake, clutching the sink, his heart pounding. The Female Spirit stood before him, her masked face a chilling reminder of the power she wielded.

"Don't expect me to rescue you every time," she said harshly, her voice a chilling echo in the confined space. "Your survival is vital to my mission."

"What do you want from me?" V demanded, frustration building within him. "Stop dropping hints!"

The spirit, her gaze piercing, lifted her hand, silencing him. "Lost in your own world?" she mocked, her voice laced with a sardonic amusement. "Time's ticking, V. Class is about to start."

V, his eyes widening, checked his watch. He bolted from the washroom, his heart pounding, the spirit's words echoing in his mind.

Ria, sitting in her classroom, studying alongside Aira, felt a shiver run down her spine. Aira signed, explaining a complex concept, her hands a blur of movement. But Ria couldn't focus. She noticed a strange aura around her classmates, a feeling reminiscent of the Male Spirit's presence, a sense of ethereal energy that made her skin crawl.

She tried to dismiss the feeling, to focus on her studies, but the classroom blurred, her head throbbing with a strange, insistent pain.

"Aira," she signed urgently, her voice laced with a growing unease, "I need to go to the washroom. I need air."

Aira, sensing her distress, nodded. Ria hurried out, her heart pounding, her senses heightened, the atmosphere feeling heavy and oppressive.

In the university corridor, Ria ran towards the washroom, her steps quick and determined. V, still shaken from his encounter with the Female Spirit, quickened his pace towards his classroom, his mind racing, his instincts telling him to escape.

They rounded a corner at the same time, colliding, their bodies a tangle of limbs and books.V looked up, surprised, his gaze meeting Ria's. He saw those familiar eyes, a flicker of recognition illuminating his face. He remembered the encounter in the car, the feeling of a connection, a bond that had been forged in the heat of a chaotic moment.

"It's you..." he said softly, a hint of surprise in his voice.

He offered to help her up, but Ria, her heart pounding, rose swiftly, avoiding his gaze. The bell rang, signaling the start of the next class. She hurried to her classroom, her footsteps echoing in the empty corridor.

V, intrigued, followed her, keeping a distance, his gaze fixed on her back. He watched as she disappeared into the classroom.

He leaned against the wall outside Ria's classroom, a faint smile gracing his lips. He watched her, a silent observer, drawn to her, captivated by her resilience.

Aira, through the classroom window, noticed V. She smoothed her hair, a mixture of admiration and calculation in her eyes. She nudged Ria, her lips forming words that held a hidden agenda.

"He's here for me?" she whispered, her voice a dangerous whisper.

The air thickened, the weight of unspoken secrets hanging heavy. Fate had brought them together, the whispers of destiny drawing them towards a collision that would forever change their lives.

CHAPTER FOURTEEN

"The Legacy of Pain"

In the evening Aira, her movements discreet and purposeful, followed V as he walked with a quiet intensity. His steps were purposeful, his gaze fixed on the dilapidated apartment building he was approaching. It was a stark contrast to the sleek, modern world he inhabited during the day.

Aira approached the building owner, a man with weathered features and eyes that held a knowing glint.

"Excuse me," she said, her voice polite, her curiosity masked by a veneer of friendliness, "Can you tell me about the man who just went in?"

The owner, his gaze lingering on Aira, studied her with a curious amusement. "You're curious about V, hmm?"

Aira's eyes widened. She hadn't known his name. "We're friends," she replied, her voice laced with a subtle lie.

The owner smiled, a knowing glint in his eyes. "You only see his smile," he said, his voice a low murmur that hinted at a deeper truth, "No one sees the pain behind it."

Aira's curiosity intensified. "What pain?" she pressed, her voice betraying a hint of concern, a concern that was genuine, yet tinged with a subtle calculation.

The owner, looking into the distance, launched into a flashback, his words painting a picture of a life marred by tragedy.

Sylvie, in modest wedding attire, entered her new home, a house that was more a gilded cage than a haven. Her husband, a man consumed by ambition and a sense of entitlement, barely acknowledged her as relatives swarmed around, their eyes filled with a mixture of disdain and curiosity.

"Well, it seems you've joined our family," her aunt sneered, her voice dripping with venom, "Some of us had our doubts."

Sylvie, her heart sinking, forced a smile, her spirit already dimmed by the icy stares that pierced her.

"Relax, dear," her uncle said, his voice laced with a condescending amusement, "We'll show you the ropes."

Sylvie knew, with a chilling certainty, that these "ropes" were not meant to guide her, but to bind her, to confine her to a life she never wanted.

Days turned into weeks, weeks into months. Sylvie's spirit, once bright and hopeful, dimmed under the constant criticism, the relentless whispers of disapproval.

"She'll never belong."

"A disgrace to our legacy."

Sylvie cried to her husband, seeking solace, seeking love, but he remained cold and distant, his heart consumed by a world far removed from her own. She realized, with a chilling clarity, that the family she had married into was ruthless, their hearts hardened by ambition and a ruthless desire for power. She feared for her unborn child, the child who carried the weight of their legacy.

Sylvie sat alone in her room, tears streaming down her face. Her relatives refused her food, punishing her for a perceived offense, their actions a cruel display of their control.

"Perhaps some decorum would earn you sustenance," her aunt sneered, her words laced with a venomous cruelty, "You and your... responsibilities."

Sylvie straightened her spine, her hand resting on her belly, a shield against their hate, a shield for her child. "Stop," she said, her voice quiet but forceful, "You will not poison him with your hatred."

She turned her back on them, walking to the window, the sight of the world beyond a fleeting glimpse of freedom. The relatives recoiled, their eyes filled with a venomous hatred, their faces twisted with rage.

Months later, Sylvie cradled her newborn son, V. Her eyes, though filled with exhaustion, held a fierce determination. She clasped a heart-shaped locket around V's neck, a symbol of her hope for a better future, a future where love would triumph over hate.

Sylvie watched V, now four years old, playing on the balcony, his laughter a joyous symphony. An uncle approached, his gaze cold and calculating.

"Sylvie, it's not safe for him to be out there," he said, his voice laced with a subtle threat.

He thrust Sylvie towards the balcony's edge. V, his innocent heart filled with terror, watched in horror as his mother fell, her scream swallowed by the wind.

In a hospital room, Sylvie lay unconscious, a frail figure, a casualty of her family's cruelty. V, clutching the locket, watched over her, tears streaming down his face. His father entered, his expression cold and dismissive.

"Father! They pushed Mother!" V cried, his voice filled with a desperate hope, a hope that was soon shattered.

"It was an accident," his father replied, his eyes cold, his words a cruel lie.

V, devastated, felt the weight of his family's betrayal, the cold indifference that had become their reality.

Years passed, a blur of bullying at school, his father's absence, and the relentless cruelty of his family. He found solace in the park, a place of shadows and solitude. But his father always caught him, his punishments harsh and brutal. The locket, a symbol of his mother's love, was broken, a tangible reminder of the pain that had consumed his life.

Ten-year-old V collapsed on the pavement, feeling faint, his body weak and fragile. Doctor John, a kind stranger, found him and took him home, a haven of unexpected kindness.

V regained consciousness, his mind filled with a confusing fog of memories. "Don't worry, son," Doctor John said, his voice gentle, his touch reassuring. "What's your name?"

"V," he whispered, his voice raspy, his body still weak.

"Could you give me your parents' number?" Doctor John asked, his gaze filled with concern.

V bowed his head, sorrow evident in his eyes. He told Doctor John about his suffering, his voice a whisper of pain, his words a testament to the cruelty he had endured. Doctor John listened with empathy, his heart aching for this young boy.

"V," Doctor John said, his voice filled with a somber tone, "I'm afraid you're very ill. You have blood cancer."

V, his world suddenly shrinking, his future uncertain, nodded, realizing his time was short, his life a fleeting flicker in the grand scheme of things. He left Doctor John's home, his heart heavy with a sadness he had learned to carry.

Nine years later, V(19) rushed to his mother's bedside. Sylvie, frail and weak, had awakened from a long coma, a flicker of life returning to her eyes.

"Mom, please... stay with me," he pleaded, his voice cracking, his heart filled with a desperate hope that was soon to be extinguished.

"V... live a fulfilling life," Sylvie whispered, her voice weak, her words filled with a profound wisdom.

"Prove those who deemed you worthless wrong. Make me proud. Become a noble gentleman.
Promise me... you'll always... protect... those you love."

V cried, his tears a torrent of grief, his heart breaking at the thought of losing his mother, the only anchor in his life. Sylvie's hand went limp, her eyes closing, her breath fading. The heart monitor flatlined.

V stood in his empty room, a room filled with the ghosts of memories, his breath ragged, his body trembling. He heard his mother's voice echoing in the silence, a whisper of encouragement, a guiding force in the darkness.

"Transform our family's story..."

His fist slammed into the wall, the sound a violent testament to his pain. He crumpled to the floor, overcome with grief, his body wracked with sobs. He clutched the broken locket, a symbol of his mother's love, and picked up a photo of her, his eyes filled with a determination that burned brighter than any sorrow.

V sat opposite the House Owner, a man who had become a beacon of kindness in his life.

"Three years already," the House Owner said, a smile gracing his lips.

"This place feels like home," V replied, his voice filled with a quiet gratitude.

"You're burning the candle at both ends," the House Owner said, his voice laced with concern, "Take care of yourself."

"There's no other way," V said, his voice firm, his determination unwavering.

"Always remember," the House Owner said, his eyes meeting V's, "You're welcome here."

"I'm enrolling in universitas," V announced, his eyes shining with a newfound hope.

The House Owner, his heart filled with pride, nodded. V, pulling out the broken locket, a symbol of a promise he couldn't break, a promise to honor his mother's legacy.

"I made her a promise," he said, his voice filled with a quiet resolve, "I won't let her down."

The flashback faded, leaving behind the lingering echo of a life marred by tragedy, a life that had been transformed by the whispers of a spirit, a spirit seeking freedom, a spirit seeking redemption.

CHAPTER FIFTEEN

"The Seeds of Friendship"

The last vestiges of daylight stretched across the street, casting long, ominous shadows, a stark contrast to the warmth that emanated from Aira. She stood outside the dilapidated building, her complexion drained of color, tears teetering on the edge of her eyelids. Beside her stood the house owner, a woman weathered by life's trials, her eyes brimming with a compassion that transcended words.

The house owner watched as V disappeared into the worn apartment building, his shoulders slumping with fatigue, his steps heavy with the weight of his burdens. She shook her head, a wistful smile gracing her lips.

"That boy carries the weight of the world on those young shoulders," she murmured, her voice filled with empathy.

She reached into her pocket and pulled out a worn photograph of a younger V, his eyes shining with a mischievous grin, his face radiating a youthful joy that seemed a distant memory now. Her gaze softened as she traced a finger over the image, a tangible connection to a past that was both cherished and lost.

Aira stood in silence, the gravity of V's narrative settling heavy on her shoulders. With each step she took away, we glimpsed fragmented flashbacks, fleeting yet potent snapshots of V's anguish.

Flashback 1: Young V, his eyes wide with horror, witnessed his mother's tragic fall from the balcony, the memory etched in his mind, a scar that would never fade.

Flashback 2: V, his face streaked with tears, watched helplessly as his mother slipped away in the hospital bed, the pain of her loss a constant companion.

Flashback 3: V, his smile strained, concealed the turmoil in his eyes, a mask of resilience that hid the pain he carried within.

The flashbacks faded, leaving Aira to continue her solitary journey, her silhouette a stark contrast against the dimming sky, her heart filled with a silent promise to help the young man who had captured her attention.

The universitas canteen buzzed with life, a cacophony of laughter and chatter, a stark contrast to V's solitude. He sat alone at a table, his gaze drawn to the vibrant energy around him, yet his face remained etched with loneliness. His empty pockets, a reminder of his financial struggles, weighed him down, a constant source of anxiety.

Aira, watching from outside, observed his silent struggle. She saw the hunger in his eyes, the way he avoided the cashier, a silent testament to his desperate need. With a gentle smile, she grabbed two trays, one filled with her usual lunch, the other laden with V's favorite foods.

Aira entered the canteen, her eyes locking with V. He started to rise, but she stopped him with a soft gesture. "Please. Stay."

V, confused, hesitated. Aira placed the tray in front of him, the aroma of the food, familiar and comforting, filling the air.

"I know you're hungry," she said, her voice soft, her words a balm to his unspoken needs.

He stared at the food, his stomach rumbling, the familiar scents arousing a pang of hunger.

Shame battled with his need, but Aira's gaze, understanding and kind, melted away his resistance. He picked up a fork, a small smile gracing his lips.

"I'm Aira," she said, extending her hand. "Can we be friends?"

V hesitated, his heart pounding with a mixture of nervousness and anticipation. Then he took her hand, his own smile widening.

"I'm V," he said, his voice a gentle murmur. "Alright, let's be friends."

V and Aira walked side by side in comfortable silence, the universitas grounds a backdrop to their burgeoning friendship. Aira stole glances at him, her admiration growing with each step. She noticed the way he walked, the kindness in his eyes, the way his brow furrowed in thought. She found herself captivated by his quiet strength, his resilience, his vulnerability.

V, oblivious to her gaze, walked with his usual quiet strength, a hint of relief softening his features as he enjoyed this unexpected companionship, a brief respite from his heavy burdens.

A montage sequence unfolded, capturing the burgeoning friendship between Aira and V, a friendship that blossomed with each shared moment:

Shopping Buddies: V helped Aira pick out clothes, offering honest opinions with a playful grin. Aira burst into laughter as V modeled a ridiculous hat, showcasing his unexpected silliness, a reminder of the light that shone beneath his stoic exterior.

Mall Adventure: V and Aira challenged each other in an aspirated game of air hockey, playful trash talk punctuating their competitive sides. Later, they shared a plate of fries, their conversation flowing easily between bites.

Sharing Secrets: Sitting on a park bench under a canopy of stars, they confided in each other, sharing dreams and anxieties, their vulnerabilities intertwined. Aira, drawn to V's quiet strength and compassion, felt her affection deepening with every shared moment.

Brotherly Concern: Aira introduced her elder brother, Aiden, to V. Aira, mentioning V's name to Aiden and Aiden's name to V, created a formal introduction. Aiden, his face obscured by the pulled V aside, his expression serious with concern. He sensed Aira's vulnerability and urged V to be a true friend, a source of strength and support. The sequence concluded with V nodding in understanding, sharing a solemn, determined glance with Aiden, both committed to supporting Aira.

Token of Friendship: Aira surprised V with a sleek new bike, a symbol of their shared adventures, a gesture of generosity that touched his heart. V, usually stoic, was visibly moved, a rare moment of pure joy lighting up his face.

Hidden Struggle: V, startled by a sudden nosebleed, quickly wiped away the blood, forcing a smile to mask his pain, determined to protect their carefree friendship.

The montage ended, with a sense of hope and warmth. Their friendship was a delicate flower blooming in the midst of adversity, a beacon of light in a world often shrouded in darkness. And as their bond deepened, a secret, a hidden truth, simmered beneath the surface, a truth that would change everything.

Aira's room, a haven of vibrant colors and carefully curated trinkets, reflected her personality—a mix of whimsy and determination. She scrolled through photos on her phone, her fingers tracing the screen, a familiar ritual that offered a brief respite from the weight of her thoughts.

She paused at a selfie, a picture of pure joy, captured during a spontaneous afternoon spent with V. Their smiles, genuine and bright, reflected a connection that had blossomed unexpectedly, a connection that had quickly become a beacon of light in her life.

CHAPTER SIXTEEN

"A DANCE OF FATE"

The universitas grounds buzzed with anticipation. Students, dressed in their finest attire, mingled excitedly, their laughter echoing through the air. V, however, sat alone on a bench, his gaze lost in thought, his mind a whirlwind of conflicting emotions. A flower, its petals delicate and fragrant, drifted down, landing softly in his lap. He smiled, remembering Ria's infectious laughter, the way her eyes sparkled with a vibrant energy that had touched his soul.

Aira, her face radiant with excitement, ran towards him. "V! Did you hear about the dance fest?" she asked, her voice filled with a contagious enthusiasm.

"Yeah," he replied, a smile gracing his lips, "Best of luck!"
"You should join!" Aira exclaimed, her eyes sparkling. "It's a couples' dance. I've already registered us. We'll be masked prince and princess!"

V's smile faded. He hesitated, considering the spotlight, the physical strain. He remembered his promise to Aira's brother, a promise to be a true friend, a source of strength for her.

"Alright," he said, his voice firm, a hint of determination in his eyes. "Let's do this."

Aira squealed with delight and ran off, her laughter echoing through the air. V stared at the flower, a symbol of beauty and hope, a reminder of Ria, his heart filled with a growing anxiety.

The backstage area of the auditorium was a flurry of activity. V, fidgeting in an elaborate prince costume, struggled with the collar. He winced at his reflection, tugging at the feathered mask, a symbol of mystery and intrigue. He glanced at the matching princess costume, a smile crossing his lips. He imagined Aira, her vibrant energy lighting up the stage, and a sense of anticipation filled him.

He scanned the crowd, searching for Aira, his smile fading. His heart pounded with a growing unease.

"Where's Aira? The performance is about to begin!" he exclaimed, his voice laced with worry.

Mournful music hung in the air, thick with the scent of incense. Aira, her face etched with grief, clutched a photo of her father, tears streaming down her cheeks.

Ria entered quietly, taking a seat beside her grieving friend, her heart heavy with empathy.

On a nearby table, a framed photo showed Aira, laughing, perched on her father's shoulders, a testament to
a love that had been lost.

Aira's gaze flicked from the photo to the clock, then to Ria. Panic rose in her eyes, her breath catching in her throat. She grabbed Ria's hands, her fingers trembling.

"Ria, you have to help me," she whispered, her voice urgent, her eyes pleading for understanding. "Please."
Ria, her brow creased with concern, watched Aira's frantic signing, her mind struggling to comprehend the urgency in her friend's plea.

"Go to the competition," Aira whispered, her voice filled with desperation. "Dance for me.
Please, Ria, I can't..."

"What?" Ria signed, her voice laced with shock, her mind reeling. "They'll know we switched!"

"No one will know," Aira pleaded, her voice filled with a desperate hope. "The masks... please, Ria. Do this for me."

Ria hesitated, torn between her confusion and Aira's desperation. She nodded, a silent promise in her eyes.

Ria, her heart pounding, rushed out of Aira's house. She didn't know what awaited her, but she wouldn't let Aira down. Her friend's desperation had ignited a fierce loyalty within her, a determination to support her in her time of need.

High above the auditorium, beyond the sight of mortals, the Female Spirit observed V, a hint of intrigue in her otherworldly gaze. Across the auditorium, the Male Spirit stood watch, his focus unwavering as he observed Ria's every move.

The curtains rose, bathing V and Ria in the glow of the stage lights, their figures poised and elegant. Their faces remained hidden behind intricate masks, adding an aura of mystery to their performance. The auditorium was engulfed in a slow, mesmerizing melody, setting the stage for the unfolding drama.

In the midst of the performance, V, unaware of Ria's true identity, danced with a newfound elegance and gentleness. His movements were imbued with a tender grace, a depth of emotion he hadn't realized he possessed. With skillful precision, he led Ria through the intricate choreography, their steps flowing seamlessly in perfect harmony.

As the zoomed in on the spirits, the once melodic music distorted, morphing into a frantic, fast-paced instrumental track. The sudden shift in rhythm added a sense of urgency and tension to the scene, heightening the audience's anticipation and signaling a change in the atmosphere.

On the rooftop, illuminated by the moon's glow, the Male and Female spirits cautiously circled each other, swords drawn, their expressions filled with apprehension. The tense atmosphere was palpable as they sized each other up, their movements calculated and wary, hinting at a deeper conflict yet to unfold.

"Identify yourself," the Female Spirit commanded, her voice laced with suspicion, "State your purpose here."

"And who might you be?" the Male Spirit responded, his voice laced with suspicion.

On the rooftop, under the moon's watchful gaze, the Male Spirit mirrored the Female's wary stance, his sword gleaming in the moonlight. Their silent standoff spoke volumes, each movement charged with suspicion and tension, the air heavy with unspoken conflict.

As V and Ria glided across the stage, their choreography echoed the mounting tension between the spirits. Their elegant dance, punctuated by the clash of swords, mirrored the escalating conflict above. Meanwhile, on the rooftop, the spirits engaged in a frenzied exchange of blows, their movements a blur of speed and aggression, reflecting the intensity of their confrontation.

V and Ria, their masked faces nearly touching, danced in perfect synchronization, their movements reflecting the proximity and intensity of the battling spirits.

Sparks flew as the Spirits' spectral swords collided in a flurry of blows. Suddenly, the clang of metal was replaced by an eerie silence. The spirits froze, their eyes locked in a shared trance.

Their swords faded, replaced by ethereal projections: two hands, one masculine, one feminine, slowly reaching out towards each other. A golden light emanated from the point where their fingertips almost touched, a visual representation of the destiny they were unknowingly bound to protect.

As the spirits clashed, their swords a blur of motion, they suddenly recoiled, their blades meeting with a clang. In that moment, their hands touched, a man's hand on the left, a woman's hand on the right, and they experienced a shared vision: two hands reaching out, side by side.

CHAPTER SEVENTEEN

"ECHOES OF STRENGTH"

The roar of the crowd was deafening, a sea of faces masked in anonymity. Ria stood center stage, the spotlight blinding, her own mask a flimsy shield against the onslaught of emotions. Fear prickled her skin, a cold sweat breaking out on her forehead. It was all too much, the weight of the masquerade, the pressure to play her part.

Then, she felt his presence beside her. V. His face, normally shrouded in weariness, was bathed in the stage light, his eyes searching hers. Recognition sparked in their shared gaze, a flicker of warmth that momentarily eclipsed the storm raging within her.

He smiled, a genuine, unguarded smile that sent a jolt through her. He had forgotten everything except her, for that brief, precious moment. The world shrank to the stage, their shared space a vacuum of silence that resonated louder than any applause.

But Ria couldn't meet his gaze. Panic choked her. He knew. He knew about Aira.

The emcee's voice droned on, a meaningless melody amidst the chaos in her mind. V reached out, his hand hovering inches from hers, the warmth radiating from him like a beacon in the darkness. But she flinched, her eyes darting around the crowd, searching for an escape.

She bolted, melting into the sea of faces, disappearing as quickly as she had appeared. V watched her go, a chill settling in his heart. Hurt. Confusion. Then, realization slammed into him, a tidal wave of understanding that threatened to drown him.

"If she was the one who danced... where's Aira?"

The words echoed in his mind as he raced through the throngs of people, his bike a blur of motion. Desperation fueled him, a gnawing fear twisting in his gut. He had to find Aira, had to make sure she was safe.

He shot down the highway, the wind whipping past his face, his lungs burning with each breath. The sun, a blinding glare in the afternoon sky, reflected off the windshield of a car approaching from the opposite direction. He swerved, barely avoiding a collision, pulling over to the side of the road, gasping for breath.

He tried to regain control of his bike, but it careened off the road, the handlebars twisting in his grip. The official vehicle of the Government officer approached, and V collided with the car, the impact throwing him into the asphalt with a sickening thud.

V groaned, waking up in a sterile hospital room. The Government officer, his face etched with concern, sat beside him.

"You're lucky to be alive, young man," the officer said, his voice a soothing balm amidst the throbbing pain in V's head.

V tried to piece together the fragments of his memory, the accident a hazy blur in his mind.

The officer assured him he was receiving excellent care, that his injuries weren't life-threatening.

The officer's eyes held a glint of curiosity, a spark of genuine interest. V, still groggy, stumbled through the story of his struggles, his mother's wish, the urgency that propelled him.

Doctor John, the man who had diagnosed V with blood cancer years ago, entered the room, his face etched with a familiar somberness.

"V," he said, his voice heavy with concern, "the tests... they aren't good."

The Government officer leaned forward, sensing V's internal struggle.

"V,I see something in you," the officer said, his voice firm, "something special. Consider a career in government service. You could make a real difference."

V was surprised by the offer, his eyes flickering between the two men. He had never considered a path beyond his own personal fight, his own quest for survival.

Doctor John interjected, "Sir, with all due respect, his health..."

But the Government officer waved him off, his gaze fixed on V. "I understand," he said, "but I have faith in V's potential."

A flicker of hope ignited within V, a tiny spark amidst the darkness of his illness. He looked back at the officer, his gaze steady.

"I'm in."

The words were a whisper, barely audible above the hum of the hospital machinery, yet they carried the weight of a promise, a determination to seize every moment, to make a difference.

Ria walked down the bustling market street, her mind consumed by the events of the previous day. The Masked Prince, the unsettling familiarity of V, and the chilling realization of Aira's absence. She was lost in her thoughts, a silent symphony of worry and anxiety, when a sudden gust of wind snatched several bills from her open purse.

Panic flooded her, her heart sinking as she watched the money flutter away, dancing through the air like fleeting dreams. She chased after the elusive cash, her steps quickening with each lost bill, her desperation growing with every passing second. She followed the wind's path, her gaze fixed on the entrance of a nearby sports coaching center, the last place she had seen the money vanish.

Stepping into the center, she scanned the room, her eyes searching for the lost bills. Among the bustling activity, she noticed a tall, athletic woman, her face framed by a thick mane of auburn hair, making her way towards her with a knowing glint in her eye.

"Searching for something?" the woman asked, her voice warm and reassuring.

With a smile, she raised the missing bills in her hand. Ria's recognition was immediate. It was the same woman she had encountered years ago, the archer who had given her a precious arrow, now a mentor at the center.

"Abi!" Ria signed, her face lighting up with surprise. "I can't believe it's you!"

Abi, however, remained oblivious to the connection, her focus solely on returning the lost money.

"Forgive me," she said, a hint of skepticism in her voice, "but have we met before?"

Ria signed eagerly, "It's me, Ria! You gave me your arrow! Remember? Years ago, at that school event. I was just a little girl then."

Abi's brows furrowed, a flicker of curiosity crossing her face. "Alright, 'Ria'," she said, her voice a playful challenge, "if you're so sure, let's put it to the test. How about a friendly duel with one of my students?" Ria's face lit up with recognition. She nodded eagerly, ready to prove her connection to the woman who had unknowingly sparked a passion within her.

Within minutes, Ria found herself standing on the archery range, facing one of Abi's students. Her stance was firm, her hand steady as she gripped the bow. With each arrow she released, her confidence grew, the years of practice paying off. She won the duel, her victory a testament to her talent and her unwavering determination.

Abi's eyes widened in recognition, a warm smile spreading across her face. "Oh, Ria!" she exclaimed, her voice tinged with genuine affection. "It really is you! My dear girl, you've grown up so beautifully – and your talent is even more impressive."

She enveloped Ria in a heartfelt embrace, the warmth radiating from her a balm to Ria's soul. As they reconnected, Abi's smile gradually faded, replaced by a somber expression as she recounted her own tumultuous journey with the national archery team.

Abi threw a stack of medals onto the table, the clatter of metal echoing her frustration. She ran a hand through her hair, her face etched with weariness.

"Years of training," she said, her voice bitter, "years of sacrifice. And for what? To be sidelined, manipulated, betrayed."

She shook her head sadly, "They don't want women to succeed, Ria. They fix matches, manipulate rankings, and crush anyone who dares to challenge their authority. It's all about money and power, never about fairness or talent."

Ria's expression shifted from empathy to indignation as she listened to Abi's story. The injustices Abi endured resonated deeply with Ria, her features hardening with anger. It was a narrative all too familiar for women in sports, particularly those who came from disadvantaged backgrounds.

Ria's signing became rapid and forceful, her anger evident even without understanding the words. Abi listened, her expression a mix of admiration and apprehension.

"It's a dangerous game, Ria," she said, her voice laced with caution, "they'll stop at nothing."

Ria grabbed her bow, her movements sharp and precise as she nocked an arrow. She drew back the bowstring, her gaze fixed on the target with unwavering intensity.

"They won't break me," she signed, her voice firm, "I won't let them."

She released the arrow. It hit the bullseye with a resounding thud.

"I'll show that when a woman thinks, she not only changes her own destiny but also that of others," she signed, her gaze unwavering.

Moved by Ria's passion and the familiar echoes of her own struggles, Abi nodded in agreement.

A silent pact formed between them, fueled by a shared sense of justice and a burning desire to level the playing field, not just for themselves but for all women in sports. They were two women, bound by a shared history, a shared struggle, and a shared destiny.

And they were ready to fight.

CHAPTER EIGHTEEN

"The Rose of Revelation"

The scent of polished wood, a blend of cedar and varnish, hung heavy in the air. The rhythmic "thwack" of arrows reverberated through the archery center, each strike a testament to Ria's unwavering focus. She was a blur of motion, her movements a graceful ballet of power and precision. Each arrow found its mark with deadly accuracy, sinking into the bullseye with a satisfying thud.

Abi, her coach, watched with a gentle smile, a silent observer to Ria's blossoming talent. A wave of pride washed over her as she witnessed the young archer's dedication, her determination etched on her face, glistening with sweat.

Outside, V stood mesmerized, his gaze glued to Ria's every movement. His heart pounded against his ribs, a frantic rhythm echoing the rapid thrum of his pulse. He held a single red rose, its crimson petals a stark contrast against his calloused hand. He longed to approach, to share in her triumph, to offer a word of encouragement, but a crippling wave of hesitation held him back.

The sleek silver of Aira's car pulled up, its headlights cutting through the gathering dusk. V's heart sank like a stone in a well.

Ria emerged from the training center, her face flushed with exertion, a satisfied smile gracing her lips. Aira rushed towards her, tears streaming down her cheeks. They embraced, a silent language of love and concern passing between them, their shared grief palpable in the air.

V watched, a knot of longing and loss tightening in his chest. The sight of Aira(28) handing Ria a credit card, a gesture of unspoken support, shattered the fragile hope that had flickered within him.

As Aira drove away, Ria turned, her eyes scanning the parking lot, searching for something, someone. V, hidden behind a pillar, held his breath. She didn't see him. Her gaze lingered on the empty space where Aira's car had been, a flicker of concern passing over her face.

V stepped forward, a sigh escaping his lips. He laid the rose gently on the ground, its petals wilting in the growing darkness. The unspoken words, the unspoken pain, hung heavy in the air.

He stood frozen, disbelief washing over him like a cold wave. Aira, Ria's friend, had just left.

The revelation added another layer of complexity to an already bewildering situation. His mind raced, a whirlwind of questions battling for attention.

He was trying to piece together the puzzle, to make sense of the conflicting emotions swirling within him, when his phone buzzed, Aira's name flashing on the screen.

"Hello?" V answered, his voice tinged with apprehension.

"V, thank you for being my friend," Aira's voice, choked with sadness, echoed through the phone. "Every moment with you has meant the world to me."

"What's wrong?" V asked, concern lacing his words.

"I'm leaving, V. I'm going abroad to study. I'll miss you. Goodbye, take care," Aira's voice cracked, a finality settling over her words.

"Goodbye, Aira. Take care," V replied, a sense of loss settling in his chest.

V ended the call, his gaze lingering on the empty space where Aira's car had stood just moments before. A torrent of questions swirled within him, each one a desperate plea for understanding. He yearned to reach out to Aira, to delve into the enigma that was

Ria, but he sensed that now was not the time.

He turned back to the entrance of the archery center, the rose weighing heavily in his hand.Thoughts swirled in his mind, a tempest of emotions threatening to overwhelm him.

"She's incredible," he thought, his voice a hushed whisper in the quiet night. "So focused, so driven." He looked at the rose, then back to Ria, a flicker of doubt casting a shadow over his admiration.

"But what do I really know about her?"

The memory of Aira's tearful farewell lingered in his mind, the poignant exchange between the two women etched in his memory.

"There's a whole world she lives in that I know nothing about," he mused, a sense of longing filling him. "Her struggles...her dreams..."

A wave of realization washed over him, a chilling truth hitting him like a physical blow.

"I don't even know her name."

He gazed at the rose once more, its delicate petals now tinged with a sense of hollowness, a stark reminder of his own unawareness.

"This is foolish," he conceded, his voice a resigned sigh. "I've been captivated by an image, not a person. This isn't fair to her, or to me."

He released the rose from his grasp, watching as it descended to the ground, its petals drifting away on the wind. With a heavy heart, he pivoted on his heel and strode away, departing from the archery center and from the enigmatic presence of Ria.

The abandoned rose rested on the pavement, its beauty juxtaposed against the harsh

concrete. Suddenly, an ethereal hand, belonging to a female spirit, emerged unseen, gently retrieving the

forsaken flower.

CHAPTER NINETEEN

"A Shadow of Threat"

Five years had passed, a lifetime in the realm of ambition and dreams. The walls of the archery center, once bare and echoing with the quiet hum of anticipation, now buzzed with a vibrant energy. Trophy cases, adorned with gleaming medals and framed accolades, chronicled Ria's meteoric rise to success.

Standing at the line, a seasoned veteran now, Ria's(28) concentration was a tangible force. Her posture, honed through years of unwavering dedication, exuded precision and power. Each movement was a whisper of her relentless pursuit of excellence. The tension in the air was palpable, the hum of the crowd a symphony of anticipation. It was the final district-level match, the gateway to the coveted state championship. Victory here meant a step closer to her ultimate dream.

Outside, on a bustling street, a different kind of tension hung in the air. V(28) who had once been captivated by Ria's talent, walked with a weary slouch, his shoulders burdened with defeat. The air around him felt thick with disappointment, the weight of his latest setback pressing heavily on his heart. Moments ago, he'd received the results of his government exam – another unsuccessful attempt.

"Five attempts down, one to go," he muttered to himself, his voice a hollow echo of his dwindling hope. "If I fail again..."

His thoughts trailed off, the image of Ria, her intense focus, the spark in her eyes when she hit a bullseye, momentarily lifting the weight of his disappointment. But the fleeting memory couldn't erase the sting of his latest failure.

He reached his building, the familiar steps leading him to his door. His movements were mechanical, devoid of the usual energy that once marked his stride. He unlocked the door, the click of the lock a stark reminder of his present reality.

The insistent ring of the doorbell startled him. He opened the door, expecting to see a neighbor, but the doorstep was empty. A small gift box sat perched on the welcome mat, a curious object in the otherwise mundane scene. He picked it up, curiosity piqued, his gaze lingering on the neatly tied ribbon.

He carried the box inside, his thoughts lingering on the mystery it presented. As he lifted the lid, his eyes widened in surprise. Nestled within layers of tissue paper, lay a ticket. His heart skipped a beat as he read the bold lettering: "FINAL CITY LEVEL SELECTION ARCHERY COMPETITION."

A surge of excitement, a long-dormant spark, flared within him. He recognized the significance of the ticket. It was an invitation, a chance encounter with fate, a possible reunion with Ria. The worries of his exam faded into the background, replaced by a surge of exhilaration and hope.

He couldn't quite explain the pull he felt, the irresistible allure of the event. Perhaps it was the nostalgia, the memory of that captivating encounter, or the lingering hope that had refused to die. Whatever it was, it ignited a fire within him, a burning desire to witness Ria's triumph, to reconnect with the woman who had once held his gaze captive.

The archery center buzzed with a vibrant energy, the atmosphere electric with anticipation. V took a seat in the stands, his gaze drawn to Ria. He watched her every movement, from the slight adjustments of her shoulders to the resolute tilt of her jaw. She exuded a newfound confidence, a beauty that surpassed his memories of her. Her grace and focus were a testament to her dedication, a dedication that echoed in the quiet determination etched on her face.

Time seemed to slow as Ria released her final arrow. It arced through the air, a blur of feathers and steel, before finding its mark – dead center in the bullseye. The crowd held its breath, the tension palpable in the air. Then, a hush fell over the stadium, followed by an eruption of thunderous applause.

Ria lowered her bow, a tired but triumphant smile spreading across her face. From the stands, V watched, his heart pounding in his chest, his own silent cheer drowned out by the roar of the crowd, yet no less powerful.

Ria emerged from the center, a radiant aura of victory surrounding her. V's hand tightened around the armrest, his conflicting emotions evident in his tense posture. He yearned to approach her, to offer his congratulations, but a wave of uncertainty held him back.

Ria turned to leave, heading towards the exit, her graceful steps drawing his eyes. V rose from his seat, his heart pounding in his chest, a surge of determination urging him to follow. He took a step, then stopped, his gaze lingering on her retreating figure. The crowd surged between them, obscuring her from view. V sank back into his seat, a sigh escaping his lips.

He resolutely remained in his seat, his gaze following her down the street. A mix of emotions played across his face, a poignant smile tinged with a hint of sadness. This moment belonged to her, he decided. He'd stay in the shadows, content to admire her from afar, a silent witness to her triumph.

Suddenly, his gaze sharpened, his senses tingling with an urgent alarm. He observed a group of men shadowing Ria, their demeanor ominous, their movements calculated. His instincts flared, recognizing the danger lurking beneath their facade. Something was amiss.

A surge of determination overcame him. He rose from his seat and began to follow the suspicious group, maintaining a cautious distance. They disappeared into a narrow alley, their figures blending into the shadows. Despite the trepidation gnawing at his insides, V pressed forward, venturing into the darkness, his heart hammering with a potent blend of apprehension and resolve.

The alley was dark and narrow, the air thick with the stench of dampness and decay. As he moved deeper into the shadows, his eyes adjusted to the dim light, revealing a lone figure standing at the alley's end, engaged in a hushed conversation on his phone.

Without hesitation, V moved towards him, a swiftness born from a sudden urgency. He lunged forward, clutching the man's arm and forcefully pivoting him around.

"Who are you? Why are you following her?" V's voice was urgent, laced with apprehension.

The man shoved V backward, a snarl twisting his face. As if on cue, the remaining members of the group emerged from the shadows, their countenances etched with grim determination.

V backed away, his eyes darting between the menacing figures. He raised his hands defensively, his voice shaky.

"Look, I don't like to fight!"

His words were barely audible, drowned out by the rush of adrenaline coursing through his veins.

He stumbled, a wave of dizziness hitting him, his hand flying to his head. He leaned against the wall, his knuckles white as he fought to stay upright, his face drained of color. The mercenaries exchanged cruel smiles, sensing his vulnerability.

He stumbled again, his legs giving way beneath him. The ground rushed up to meet him, and he fell, sinking into the darkness as his consciousness slipped away.

The alley was silent, the air thick with anticipation. V lay sprawled on the gritty pavement, his face pale and drawn. The mercenaries, their expressions twisted with cruel amusement, encircled him. One of them, wielding a switchblade, crouched down, the metallic glint catching the dim streetlight.

"Seems like this one's learned their lesson," the mercenary said with a sneer.

The mercenary leader's snarl turned into a yelp of surprise as a force slammed his arm back, the switchblade clattering to the pavement. He cried out in pain, clutching his elbow, his face contorted with a mixture of shock and agony.

"What in the blazes was that?" he gasped, his voice laced with fear. "Did you catch a glimpse of something?"

The other mercenaries exchanged bewildered glances, their expressions morphing from arrogant swagger to apprehensive uncertainty. The air in the alley suddenly felt different, colder, thick with an unseen tension. A metallic tang filled the air, a scent of fear and impending doom, and the echo of laughter danced on the wind.

"I didn't see a blooming' thing...did you?" Mercenary 2 asked, his voice a nervous tremor.

The lid of the nearby trash can, suddenly and inexplicably, ripped free. It spun through the air, a metallic disc flashing in the dim light, before hurtling towards the group. The men scrambled, their shouts echoing in the confined space, a chorus of panicked cries. The lid screeched past their heads, barely missing their faces, leaving a chilling whisper of wind in its wake.

They scrambled backward, their movements frantic, their eyes darting around the alley, searching for a source of the attack. One of them, his fear overriding his caution, swung a wild punch at the empty air. He connected with nothing but emptiness, his fist barely meeting resistance before he stumbled forward, losing his balance. He tripped over a stack of discarded tires, crashing onto the pavement with a sickening thud, his cry of pain muffled by the sudden rush of fear that choked his throat.

A crowbar, clutched tightly in one of the mercenary's hands, suddenly wrenched free, sending the man stumbling backward. He hit the wall with a thud, the crowbar clattering to the ground, leaving him disoriented and stunned. His eyes darted around the alley, searching for the source of the attack, a sense of dread replacing the initial arrogance.

A nearby chain, hanging from a rusty hook, suddenly whipped out, coiling around the ankle of another mercenary. He shrieked in terror, falling to the ground, the chain tightening around his leg,cutting off circulation. The cold, metallic grip sent a jolt of pain through his ankle, a sharp reminder of the unseen force that had them trapped.

The alley was a whirlwind of movement, a cacophony of sounds. The air was thick with the scent of fear, a metallic tang lingering in the air. The mercenaries scrambled, their movements frantic, their eyes wide with terror. They swung wildly, their fists connecting with nothing but empty air.

The discarded wooden pallet, leaning against the wall, suddenly tipped over, crashing down with a force that sent the mercenary cowering behind it. He was trapped, pinned against the wall, the pallet pressing against his chest, cutting off his breath.

"R-Run! Get out of here!" The mercenary leader stuttered, his voice choked with terror.

They scrambled to their feet, their movements frantic and disorganized. They fled blindly into the night, their figures vanishing into the shadows, their panicked cries echoing in the darkness.

The Female Spirit, her form still unseen, watched them retreat, a mischievous smile playing on her lips. A cold breeze, carrying the scent of honeysuckle and the echo of her laughter, swept through the alley.

"Cowards," she chuckled softly, her voice a whisper on the wind.

She turned her gaze to V, still lying unconscious on the ground. Her expression softened, a wave of concern washing over her ethereal features. With a gentle touch, she lifted V into her arms, his form weightless against her ethereal presence. A soft shimmer enveloped them, a swirl of light and shadow, and then they vanished, leaving behind only a faint trace of their presence.

The air hung heavy with the lingering echoes of their chaotic departure. The scent of fear and desperation mingled with the dampness of the alley, a stark reminder of the unseen forces at play.

Meanwhile, in a brightly lit hospital room, a different kind of urgency prevailed. Dr. John, a seasoned medical professional, pored over a patient's chart, his face etched with concern. Every line and notation drew his full attention, his dedication evident in the furrow of his brow and the intensity of his gaze.

Dr. John's eyes widened in surprise as a figure materialized on the vacant hospital bed. It was V, lying motionless and pale. The doctor's grip on the patient chart loosened as he rushed to V's side, his expression etched with deep concern and urgency.

"How on earth did he...? Never mind," he muttered to himself, his voice laced with apprehension. "We need to stabilize him, quickly."

Dr. John sprang into action, his skilled hands swiftly assessing V's condition and initiating treatment. With practiced efficiency, he maneuvered through the medical procedures, his focus unwavering despite the urgency of the situation.

In the corner of the room, unnoticed by anyone else, the Female Spirit fixed her gaze on V.
Her eyes, filled with an enigmatic intensity, held a secret, a silent promise that hovered in the air like a
whispered promise.

CHAPTER TWENTY

"A Shadow Falls"

Ria's strides were long and determined, her pace quickening as she navigated the city streets. A sense of urgency pulsed through her, a silent alarm ringing in her heart. She cast a wary glance over her shoulder, a flicker of unease dancing across her features. The shadows, elongated by the setting sun, played tricks on her eyes, but she couldn't shake the feeling of being watched.

Three figures, their silhouettes menacing against the fading light, materialized in the distance. They were the same ominous figures who had stalked her in the alley, their presence a chilling echo of the violence she had narrowly escaped. The metallic tang of fear, the sharp scent of danger, filled her senses.

Her heart pounded in her chest, a frantic rhythm mirroring the rapid thrum of her pulse. She broke into a sprint, her footfalls echoing against the pavement, her breaths coming in short gasps. The mercenaries, their faces hardened with determination, gave chase.

She veered into a narrow side street, the fading light casting long, distorted shadows, creating a labyrinth of darkness. The sound of tires screeching on asphalt echoed behind her, a car hurtling around the corner, its headlights piercing the gathering gloom. Desperation fueled her flight, her legs burning, her lungs screaming for air.

The car, a sleek black sedan, collided with Ria, the impact echoing with a sickening thud. She was flung onto the pavement, her body crumpling against the unforgiving concrete. Her vision blurred, a wave of dizziness washing over her. The world spun, the city lights blurring into a dizzying kaleidoscope of color.

The mercenaries halted, their eyes fixed on the vehicle, their expressions a mixture of surprise and annoyance. The car door swung open, revealing Aiden(29), Aira's estranged elder brother, stepping out with a commanding presence. His impeccably tailored suit, a stark contrast to the gritty alley, seemed to radiate affluence and authority. With every step, Aiden exuded a chilling ruthlessness, his piercing gaze conveying a power that made the mercenaries shrink back.

"Boss, there she is," Mercenary 1 said, his voice laced with a chilling smirk, pointing to Ria's motionless form.

Aiden strode forward, his cold eyes fixed on Ria, his movements slow and deliberate, a predator approaching his prey. The dimming sunlight cast harsh shadows on his face, emphasizing the cruel contours around his mouth. His smile was a chilling imitation of kindness, a mask hiding the ruthlessness beneath.

"Finally, I've got you," Aiden said, his voice a smooth melody, laced with a deadly undercurrent.

His laughter, a chilling symphony of malice, filled the air, echoing through the silent streets.

The mercenaries fidgeted uneasily, exchanging wary looks as dusk descended, casting long shadows across the scene.

"What do we do with her now, boss?" Mercenary 2 asked, his voice trembling slightly.

Aiden's smile twisted into a cruel smirk. He knelt beside Ria, his gaze fixed on her face, his eyes reflecting a twisted satisfaction. He ground his heel into her hand, the sickening crunch of bone echoing in the silence. Ria's muffled scream was swallowed by the city's relentless hum.

One of the mercenaries presented Aiden with a heavy metal rod, its surface reflecting the dim streetlight. Aiden accepted it, gauging its weight with a cruel smirk. He raised the rod, the streetlight glinting off its surface, then brought it down with brutal force. The sound of shattering bone echoed in the sudden silence, a sharp, piercing sound that sliced through the night. Ria's body went limp, her face contorted in agony.

As darkness threatened to engulf her, she caught a fleeting glimpse – a woman's face, framed by the car window, observing her with an inscrutable expression. Then, oblivion descended, her senses fading into a dark abyss.

The mercenary leader strode forward, his features drained of color in the waning light, a silent foreboding shadow looming over the scene.

"Boss, there's another problem," he said, his voice trembling. "What happened in the alley...?"

Aiden whirled around, his eyes blazing with fury, his anger palpable in the tense air. His hand tightened around the metal rod, his knuckles turning white with tension.

"What the hell happened?" he roared, his voice low and deadly. "Where are the others? I trusted you with this job, and you've failed me. Now, I have to clean up your mess myself. My money was supposed to ensure this job was done, but it seems it was all for nothing, wasn't it?"

The Mercenary Leader froze, his voice caught in his throat. The shadow of fear, a chilling presence, hovered in the air.

Aiden swung the metal rod with brutal force, striking the Mercenary Leader's skull, ending his existence in an instant. The mercenary fell to the ground, his body still for the first time in his life.

Aiden and the remaining mercenaries vanished into the night, their figures blending seamlessly with the encroaching darkness, abandoning Ria's battered form to the unforgiving streets. The echo of their footsteps faded into the symphony of city sounds, leaving behind a chilling silence.

Moments passed, the streetlights casting long, dancing shadows, before a glimmer of light unveiled the Male Spirit kneeling beside Ria. Anguish etched his face as he surveyed her injuries, the harsh reality of her shattered hand illuminated by the flickering streetlights.

"It's my fault," he whispered, his voice filled with self-reproach. "I was supposed to protect you."

He gently lifted Ria, his form shimmering as he carried her into the night. The streetlights cast long, dancing shadows around them as they vanished into the darkness, leaving behind only the faintest whisper of their presence, a silent promise of retribution.

The city, with its relentless hum, swallowed their disappearance, its shadows concealing their fate. But in the hearts of those who witnessed the scene, a spark of hope ignited, a promise of justice, a yearning for the balance to be restored.

The stage was set, the players assembled, the conflict brewing. The threads of fate, woven with violence and betrayal, were tightening, the battle for Ria's fate about to begin.

CHAPTER TWENTY-ONE

"TOGETHER WHISPERS"

The sterile white of the hospital room seemed to amplify the grim reality of Ria's situation. The harsh fluorescent lights cast a cold, uncaring glare on her face, highlighting the stark lines of pain etched across her features. The doctor, his expression etched with concern, examined her mangled hand, his fingers tracing the lines of the shattered bone.

"She'll be okay," he said to the nurse, his voice a somber melody. "But...she's lost the use of her hand. The damage is too extensive."

His words hung heavy in the air, a stark reminder of the cruel hand of fate. The doctor's gaze lingered on Ria, his empathy palpable in the air. But for all his medical expertise, he couldn't erase the pain, the profound loss she had suffered.

The Male Spirit, unseen by the doctor and nurse, lingered in the corner of the room, his spectral form shimmering with a sorrowful aura. His heart was heavy with guilt, a wave of self-reproach washing over him. He had failed to protect Ria, to shield her from harm.

His gaze lingered on her, a silent promise of vengeance burning in his eyes. He couldn't erase the pain she had endured, but he could seek retribution. He could ensure that those responsible for this act of violence would face their own reckoning.

In another room, a different kind of pain played out. V, his face pale and gaunt, lay in his hospital bed, the sterile white sheets a stark contrast to his vibrant life. Dr. John, his face etched with concern, stood beside the bed, the weight of his diagnosis heavy on his heart.

"His leukemia," Dr. John said, his voice a hushed whisper, "it's aggressive. He needs constant care, round-the-clock treatment...He's...running out of time."

The Female Spirit sat beside V, her ethereal form shimmering with a sorrowful aura. Her eyes, filled with compassion, reflected the pain of his struggle. She had watched over him, protecting him from the shadows that threatened to consume him. But even her power was not enough to stop the relentless march of disease.

A sudden, strange energy pulsed through the air, a connection that drew the spirits together, a silent call across the vast expanse of the hospital. They met in a darkened hallway, their forms solidifying as they faced each other. The fluorescent lights, buzzing overhead, cast a ghostly glow on their spectral forms.

The tension between them crackled like static electricity, a silent tension that filled the air with unspoken words, unspoken emotions.

"Someone is orchestrating this," the Male Spirit said, his voice low and intense, his eyes reflecting a growing sense of urgency. "Targeting them both."

The Female Spirit hesitated, her masked gaze fixed on the floor. She raised her hand, a spectral flame flickering in her palm, casting an eerie glow on her features.

"But why?" she asked, her voice laced with uncertainty. "What could they possibly gain?"

The Male Spirit stepped closer, his spectral form shimmering with urgency. He reached out, his hand hovering inches from hers.

"We need to find out," he said, his voice a hushed whisper, a plea for understanding. "Together."

The Female Spirit stared at his outstretched hand, a hesitant flicker of hope sparking within her. She slowly, reluctantly, extended her own, the flames in her palm dying down, replaced by a faint, pulsing glow as their hands met.

A shared sense of purpose, a silent understanding, pulsed through the air. They were bound together by a common purpose, a shared destiny.

The Male Spirit, however, felt a different emotion, a deep-seated mistrust, a lingering suspicion of the Female Spirit. He extended his hand, palm open, a gesture of truce, a desperate attempt to bridge the chasm that separated them.

But the Female Spirit, her eyes narrowing, drew back, her grip tightening around the hilt of her spectral sword. She was wary of his intentions, his motives unclear, his past shrouded in mystery.

The Male Spirit lowered his hand slowly, shoulders slumping with a sigh. He understood her distrust, her reluctance to trust. For now, their shared mission was all that mattered. They must unravel the mystery behind the attacks, the shadowy forces that threatened their own kind, and ensure that V and Ria had a chance at a future, however uncertain it may be.

They stood there, their forms shimmering in the flickering light, two spirits bound by destiny, their path ahead shrouded in uncertainty, their purpose unwavering. The battle for their world, for the lives of those they had sworn to protect, had begun.

CHAPTER TWENTY-TWO

"The Archer's Fury"

Ria's eyes fluttered open, the pain in her head a sharp, throbbing reminder of the violence she had endured. She winced as the harsh fluorescent light of the hospital room assaulted her senses. She tentatively flexed her fingers, a wave of nausea washing over her as she saw the mangled, swollen mess of her hand. Tears welled up, blurring her vision, but she quickly blinked them away, a steely resolve hardening her features.

She threw back the covers, ignoring the dizziness that washed over her. She swung her legs to the floor, gritting her teeth, her gaze fixed on the door. The pain, the betrayal, the fear, ignited a burning anger within her. She had been attacked, her life threatened, her dreams shattered. She wouldn't succumb to despair. She would fight back.

She left the hospital, the crisp morning air stinging her lungs, the weight of her injury a constant reminder of the violence she had endured. But her spirit, her determination, remained unbroken.

She stood at the entrance to the archery training center, her heart heavy with dread. This was her sanctuary, the place where she honed her skills, where she dreamt of greatness, where she found solace. But today, the air hung heavy with a terrible silence.

She pushed the door open, the sound a jarring intrusion into the eerie quietude that had settled over the training center. It was usually bustling with activity, a symphony of arrows striking targets, a of hope and ambition. But today, it was eerily empty, the air thick with a sense of foreboding.

Then she saw him – her coach, Abi, lying motionless on the floor. Ria rushed to his side, her knees buckling as she fell beside him, her body trembling with a mix of shock and despair. She cradled Abi's lifeless body in her arms, sobs wracking her frame, her cries echoing through the empty space.

Her gaze fell on the shattered trophies, the ripped photographs, the scattered medals – all symbols of her dreams, now seemingly as broken as her fingers. The weight of betrayal, the enormity of the loss, crashed over her, a wave of grief threatening to consume her.

Suddenly, a sharp blow to the back of her head plunged her into darkness.

Ria's eyes fluttered open. She was bound to a chair, her head lolling against the rough wood. The room was sparsely furnished, with bare concrete walls and flickering fluorescent lights. A group of mercenaries, their faces hardened and watchful, stood around her.

A man in a crisp suit, his smile a chilling mask concealing the ruthlessness beneath, stepped forward.

"Hello, Ria," he said, his voice a smooth, chilling melody. "Your reputation precedes you."

He gestured to his mouth, signaling that he knew she could read lips. He then placed a document on the table in front of her.

"Sign this," he said, his voice calm but firm. "It's a statement declaring your withdrawal from the upcoming national archery championship."

Ria stared at him, her eyes blazing with defiance, even as tears streamed down her face. She shook her head vehemently, refusing to sign the document. Her spirit, her will, remained unbroken.

A mercenary, his expression twisted with cruelty, grabbed her by the hair, yanking her head back. Ria winced, but her gaze never wavered.

"Listen," the man in the suit said, his voice growing colder. "The only purpose is that my...another...boss needs this championship. You understand?"

Ria's blood ran cold as the motive behind the attacks became clear – they wanted her out of the competition. They wanted to silence her, to crush her dreams. She shook her head fiercely, refusing to sign, refusing to surrender.

"This is your last chance," the man said, his voice laced with a chilling threat. "Sign the document, or..."

He let the threat hang in the air, a silent promise of violence. But Ria's defiance didn't waver. Her gaze remained locked onto his, a challenge burning in her eyes.

"Fine," he snapped, his frustration evident in his tone. "You've made your choice."

He turned to the mercenaries, his jaw clenched. "Get rid of her."

He strode out of the room, leaving Ria at the mercy of the mercenaries. Their shadows loomed over her, growing longer and more menacing in the flickering light.

The mercenary's knife descended towards Ria, his face twisted with cruelty. Suddenly, he convulsed, a guttural scream ripping from his throat. His eyes rolled back, vacant and terrifying. The other mercenaries stumbled back in fear as their comrade, now possessed, spun and plunged the knife into the chest of the mercenary beside him.

The room erupted into chaos. The possessed mercenary, his movements jerky and unnatural, lashed out with brutal, inhuman strength. He grabbed a heavy chain, whipping it around like a deadly serpent, sending another mercenary crashing into the wall.

As the remaining mercenaries scrambled for their lives, the air shimmered. The Male Spirit materialized, his expression a mask of cold fury. He saw Ria, her eyes wide with fear, her spirit unbroken. A reassuring smile, a silent promise of protection, crossed his face.

"I arrived just in time," he said, his voice a calm whisper, a reassuring presence in the midst of the chaos.
Ria stared, speechless, as the Male Spirit raised his hand. An

invisible force, a surge of power emanating from his form, blasted a mercenary across the room, sending him crashing into a table. The remaining mercenaries, realizing they were outmatched, made a desperate break for the door.

The possessed mercenary, fueled by the Male Spirit's power, hurled a heavy metal object – a wrench – at their fleeing forms. The wrench caught one of the mercenaries squarely in the back of the head, sending him sprawling to the floor.

The other mercenaries escaped into the hallway, abandoning their fallen comrades. The possessed mercenary, the unnatural energy draining from him, collapsed, his body finally at peace.

The Male Spirit stood, his gaze fixed on Ria. The room fell into an eerie silence, broken only by the groans of the injured mercenaries.

Suddenly, Raju burst into the room, his eyes wide with shock and fury. He stared at the carnage, at Ria's unconscious form, his plans in ruins.

"She...she's gone!" he cried, his voice a strangled whisper.

His face drained of color as he spun on his heel and bolted, his panicked footsteps echoing down the hallway. He stumbled over his own feet in his haste to escape, adding to the frantic urgency of his flight.

Raju stumbled into an opulent room, his clothes disheveled, his face drained of color with fear. He stood before a powerful-looking man, the Aiden, who sat behind a massive mahogany desk.

"Boss... I... I'm sorry... she escaped..." Raju stuttered, his voice trembling.

The Aiden slammed his hand on the desk, the force of the blow reverberating through the room. He rose, his face contorted with rage. His shadow, a looming presence, seemed to engulf Raju. A vein throbbed in his temple, his silence more menacing than any shout. With a swift, brutal backhand, he struck Raju across the face. Raju crumpled to the floor, whimpering, cradling his jaw, the fear in his eyes palpable.

"I...I don't understand," Raju stammered, grappling for words to articulate the inexplicable events he had just experienced. "There was...something..."

The Aiden fixed him with a steely gaze, the intensity of his stare piercing through Raju like icy daggers.

Raju, his face bruised, dropped to his knees before the Aiden, his eyes pleading for forgiveness.

"She got away...but we'll find her," he whispered, his voice desperate. "I swear it. Just tell me what you want me to do!"

He groveled at the Aiden's feet, his hands shaking as he reached out to touch the hem of the Aiden's expensive suit.

The Aiden stared down at him, his face an impassive mask, leaving Raju trembling with uncertainty and fear.

The Aiden paced, his mind churning with thoughts, crafting a new strategy. A WOMAN , her face hidden in the shadows, leaned forward, her breath catching in her throat as she eavesdropped on the conversation. A diamond bracelet on her wrist glinted in the dim light, catching a stray tear that rolled down her cheek. She watched, her heart heavy with a mix of fear and hope, as the Aiden plotted his next move.

The battle lines had been drawn, the stakes raised. The fight for Ria's life, for her freedom, had only just begun. The forces of darkness were closing in, their motives shrouded in mystery, their power formidable. But Ria, fueled by anger and a fierce determination to survive, was ready to fight back. And she wouldn't be alone.

The unseen forces, the spirits, were aligning themselves, their destinies intertwined with Ria's. The clash of wills, the struggle for control, was about to reach a fever pitch. The stage was set, the players in place, the game about to begin.

CHAPTER TWENTY-THREE

"THE ARCHER'S RETURN"

Moonlight bathed Ria's tear-stained face as she slept fitfully, her injured hand clutched to her chest, a silent testament to the violence she had endured. The Male Spirit hovered beside her, his spectral form shimmering in the pale light. His expression was a shifting mix of sorrow and determination, a silent promise to protect her, to ensure she would not be a victim again.

Ria sat up, a wave of nausea washing over her as she remembered the events of the previous days. Her gaze fell on her mangled hand, the pain a dull ache, but the reality of her injury hit her with renewed force. She recalled Abi, her coach, lying lifeless on the floor of the training center, her mentor, her friend, her source of inspiration, gone. The fear, the raw terror, of facing Raju and his men, still clung to her like a shroud.

She curled up on the bed, her body wracked with sobs. The weight of her shattered dreams, the loss of her mentor, the uncertainty of her future – it all crashed down upon her, threatening to drown her in despair.

The Male Spirit observed her, his heart aching for her pain. He couldn't bear to see her suffer, to witness her spirit crumble. Reaching out with his spectral hand, he gently caressed her forehead, a wave of calming energy washing over Ria. Her sobs subsided into gentle, even breaths. She fell into a deep, peaceful sleep, her face finally relaxed, the tension leaving her features.

The Male Spirit sat beside her, his ethereal form shimmering in the moonlight. He watched over her, a silent guardian, his own heart heavy with worry. He had failed to protect her completely, but he would not fail her again.

He reached out, a spectral hand hovering over her, his fingertips glowing faintly. Hesitantly, he brushed a stray tear from her cheek. His touch brought a momentary calm to her expression, but her brow remained furrowed in her sleep. The pain, the fear, the uncertainty, lingered beneath the surface.

The next day night, Ria walked home, her arms laden with grocery bags. The streetlights cast long shadows around her, intensifying the sense of vulnerability she felt. A group of drunken men stumbled out of a nearby bar, their laughter echoing ominously in the night.

Their eyes fixated on Ria, predatory intentions masked poorly by their inebriated state. One of the men nudged his friend with a lecherous grin, a silent agreement passing between them. With each step, their approach became more menacing. They cornered her in a dimly lit alleyway, blocking her path with leering faces and menacing gestures.

Ria instinctively raised her hands defensively, her pulse racing with fear. One of the men reached out towards her, his alcohol-laden breath making her recoil.

Suddenly, a stone cut through the air, striking one of the men squarely on the shoulder. He cried out in pain, clutching his wounded arm, while his companions faltered, their false bravado shattered by the unexpected turn of events.

From the shadows emerged a young man, around 28, his presence commanding yet composed. Tall and athletic, his calm demeanor belied an underlying alertness to the situation unfolding before him.

"Hey, are you okay?" he asked, his voice low and reassuring.

Ria's nod was hesitant, her voice stifled by a lump in her throat.

"It's getting late," he said, his voice gentle. "Would you like me to walk you home? Just to be safe."

Ria nodded once more, her silent gratitude palpable. She led the way, the man following at a respectful distance.

As they reached her front door, Ria turned to express her thanks, but the man had disappeared. She scanned the street, a mix of confusion and disappointment clouding her features. She couldn't explain the sudden feeling of warmth, the sense of security, he had provided.

From the rooftop, the Male Spirit watched, a faint smile gracing his lips. He had orchestrated the encounter, hoping to provide Ria with a sense of comfort, a reminder that she wasn't alone.

Ria startled awake, her heart pounding in her chest. The Male Spirit materialized in her room, his sudden presence catching her off guard.

"Ria, we need to talk," he said, his voice a calm whisper. "I have a plan."

Ria signed, "What is it?" her expression a blend of curiosity and apprehension, her hands conveying the message with precision.

"I can heal your hand," the Male Spirit said, his voice tinged with hope. "Restore your fingers to normal.But it will take all my strength. I'll be weakened...maybe for a long time."

Ria's gaze locked onto his, her chest tight with anticipation. He extended his hands, the tips of his fingers emitting a soft, otherworldly glow. With intense focus, he channeled a pulsating stream of spectral energy towards the locket hanging around Ria's neck. The locket responded with a subtle hum, its surface aglow with newfound power.

A gasp escaped Ria's lips as she experienced a rush of warmth enveloping her, concentrating on her injured hand. She lowered her gaze, her eyes widening in disbelief. Her fingers lay straight, the swelling vanished, the bones restored to wholeness. She flexed them cautiously, a fleeting pang of discomfort serving as a reminder of the recent ordeal.

"I couldn't heal everything," the Male Spirit said, his voice tinged with fatigue. "The pain will linger...but you can use your hand again."

Tears brimmed in Ria's eyes as she threw herself into the Male Spirit's arms, embracing him tightly. Initially taken aback, he soon reciprocated, a tender smile gracing his features. In this silent exchange, they shared a profound understanding, their connection forged through shared sorrow and newfound hope.

The Male Spirit watched Ria as she slept, a faint smile gracing his masked features. He reached out, his spectral hand hovering over the locket on her chest, its glow pulsing softly. He retracted his hand, a hint of melancholy in his gaze. He knew that the threat against her wasn't over.

Later, Ria sat at her desk, a steely resolve reflected in her gaze. Methodically, she completed an application form for the city archery championship. Ria signed the application with a flourish, a triumphant smile on her face. She held the completed form aloft, as if savoring the weight of her decision.

Unseen, the Male Spirit watched from the shadows, his expression softening into a gentle smile. He faded away, leaving behind a faint shimmer of light.

"Remember, Ria," his voice echoed in her mind. "Never take off that locket. It's the source of your strength."

Ria nodded, her fingers instinctively finding the outline of the locket beneath her shirt. She caught her reflection in a nearby mirror. A faint smile touched her lips as she remembered the Male Spirit's words. She lifted her chin, meeting her own gaze with newfound confidence.

The archery arena buzzed with anticipation. Ria stood poised on the line, her bow steady in her grip, her eyes locked on the distant target. It's been ages since she last felt the familiar weight of her bow, the smooth pull of the arrow, the rush of adrenaline in competition. Ria winced as she drew back the bowstring, the pain shooting through her injured hand.

But she didn't falter. Her jaw set with determination, her eyes focused on the target, her body remembering the muscle memory of years of training. With a focused exhale, she released the arrow.

It cut through the air, hitting the target dead center with a satisfying thud. Shot after shot, she proved her resilience, refusing to be defeated by her injury.

As the competition concluded, Ria emerged victorious to a wave of applause. Her bittersweet smile reflected both her triumph and lingering pain, a constant reminder of her struggles. As she exited the arena, her celebration was abruptly cut short by the sight of mercenaries lurking in the shadows.Their grim faces revealed malicious intent, triggering Ria's instinct for survival.

Without hesitation, she sprinted away, the sound of their pursuit echoing through the empty arena. She ducked into a secluded storage space, her smirk revealing newfound confidence. This was her territory, and she knew how to defend it. Above, the Male Spirit watched, his concern growing with each passing moment.

Seven mercenaries advanced, a formidable wall of muscle and steel. Ria stood tall, her expression resolute, her fingers already dancing over the quiver of arrows at her back.

A Warrior Unleashed

The air crackled with anticipation. Ria stood poised, her bow steady in her grip, her eyes locked on the target. It had been too long since she'd felt the familiar weight of the bow, the smooth pull of the arrow, the rush of adrenaline. A sharp pain shot through her hand, a reminder of her recent ordeal, but she didn't falter. Her jaw clenched, her eyes laser-focused on the target, her body remembering the muscle memory of years of training.

Three mercenaries charged, their faces twisted with malice. Ria's heart hammered in her chest, her instincts taking over. She nocked an arrow, drew back the bowstring, and released in one fluid motion. The arrow sang through the air, a blur of feathers and steel, splitting the air with a sharp whistle. It struck the lead mercenary's chest, pinning him to a wooden target dummy with a sickening thud. The impact sent shockwaves through the air, silencing the mercenaries for a fleeting moment.

Ria's movements were a blur of motion. She spun, her senses heightened, her eyes taking in every detail of the arena. She fired two arrows in rapid succession, her aim unwavering. The first arrow disarmed a mercenary, his sword clattering harmlessly to the wooden floor. The second arrow, a whisper of steel and feathers, flew true, pinning the other mercenary's sleeve to a support beam, inches from his terrified face. He screamed in pain, his hand trapped, his movement restricted.

The Male Spirit surged forward, spectral energy crackling around him, ready to unleash his power. He saw Ria's unwavering gaze, her defiant stance, a silent message passing between them. She shook her head slightly, a flicker of steel in her eyes. I can handle this. The Male Spirit hesitated, his protective instincts battling with his respect for her independence. He hung back, his spectral form shimmering with restless energy, his fists clenched, his concern growing. He watched, his heart pounding with a mixture of admiration and apprehension, a haunting melody weaving through his thoughts. A fleeting vision, a woman's face shrouded in shadows, her expression filled with sorrow, gripped him, unsettling him. He shook his head, trying to clear the vision, but it lingered, a chilling reminder of the larger threat looming over them.

Ria backpedaled, her movements graceful, her focus unwavering. She fired arrow after arrow, each one a testament to her skill. She used the environment to her advantage, circling around training dummies, leaping over low benches, turning the space into a deadly obstacle course for her pursuers. She was a blur of motion, her movements precise and deadly, a warrior unleashed.

In a critical moment, Rohan appeared, his eyes flashing with concern. He rushed to Ria's aid, his own martial skills honed from years of training. Together, they fought back, their struggle a chaotic dance of survival. They moved with a fluid grace, a synergy born from shared danger and shared purpose.They ducked, dodged, and countered, their movements a blur of fists and blades, a whirlwind of action amidst the archery equipment.

With the last mercenary subdued, Ria lowered her bow, chest heaving with exertion, her eyes burning with a mixture of adrenaline and relief. Rohan approached, their shared smile a silent acknowledgment of their victory. The Male Spirit, still troubled by the vision, watched over them, his concern deepening.

"Impressive skills you have there," Rohan said, his voice filled with admiration.

Ria's smile wavered, but she managed to convey her gratitude with a shaky gesture of thanks.

"I'm Rohan," he said, his voice taking on a shy tone. "I...I've seen you compete before. I wanted to talk to you, but I...I got nervous."

Ria's gaze lingered on him, a swell of gratitude and newfound hope rising within her. The man who had come to her aid, who had defended her, was a stranger, yet he had shown her kindness in a moment of desperation.

"Friends?" Rohan asked, holding out his hand.

Ria hesitated briefly before intertwining her fingers with his. A surge of warmth coursed through her, melting away the tension in her muscles. A genuine smile graced her lips, illuminating her face with newfound light, a beacon of hope amidst the darkness.

The battle was far from over. But for now, she had her strength, her skills, and a newfound friend by her side. The shadows that had threatened to consume her were receding, replaced by a glimmer of hope, a promise of a future, however uncertain it might be. The journey ahead was fraught with danger, but she wouldn't face it alone.

CHAPTER TWENTY-FOUR

"A Spark Ignites"

One day later ,As the clock struck midnight, casting long shadows across the street, Ria emerged from the shadows of her apartment building. She saw Rohan leaning against his motorbike, a warm smile lighting up his face. He patted the seat behind him, inviting her to join.

Ria hesitated briefly, her eyes scanning the dimly lit street, before nodding. A small, hesitant smile graced her lips, a flicker of curiosity battling with a lingering sense of caution. He had come to her doorstep, a surprise visitor, his presence a comforting balm in the midst of her anxieties.

Rohan pulled up the bike near a secluded corner of the park, where shadows draped their surroundings in darkness. He dismounted, his movements confident yet inviting, and gestured for Ria to follow.

"Where are we going?" Ria signed, her brow furrowed with curiosity.

Rohan offered her a mysterious smile, gently taking her hand, and leading her further into the park. Ria, puzzled yet intrigued, allowed herself to be led, her curiosity piqued by Rohan's enigmatic demeanor.

"Look up, Ria," Rohan signed, speaking softly. "Count the stars for me."

Ria's gaze lifted to the night sky, her initial unease dissolving as she began to count the twinkling stars. The night air was crisp, carrying the scent of pine and damp earth. The world seemed tofade away, replaced by the vastness of the universe, a universe filled with infinite possibilities.

Abruptly, a resounding WHOOSH sliced through the tranquil air. A firework, a burst of light and color against the dark canvas of the sky, rocketed upwards, erupting into a dazzling spectacle. But it wasn't an ordinary display. This firework morphed into a mesmerizing tableau: an archer releasing an arrow, mirroring Ria's own prowess. Then, radiant words burst forth in sparkling brilliance:

"HAPPY BIRTHDAY RIA."

Ria gasped, her eyes widening with surprise and joy. Tears shimmered in her eyes, a mixture of joy and disbelief. She turned to Rohan, finding him observing her with a tender smile. With a trembling hand, she stepped closer to him, her fingers intertwining with his.

"Happy Birthday, Ria," Rohan signed, speaking softly.

He enfolds her in a tender embrace. Ria yielded to his arms, enveloped by a flood of warmth and gratitude.

Her heart, a symphony of emotions, swelled with joy and a newfound sense of hope. A montage unfolded, capturing the blossoming of Ria and Rohan's relationship, communicated through gestures, expressions, and the subtle language of shared moments:

Ria stood on a podium, her chest swelling with pride as a gold medal adorned her neck.Amidst the cheering crowd, she signed "Thank you" to Rohan, her eyes gleaming with gratitude.

Another competition, another victory. Ria ascended the podium once more, her smileradiant as she signed "We did it!" to Rohan, their shared triumph palpable.

Ria and Rohan shared tender moments as they navigated everyday life. They laughedtogether while grocery shopping, playfully bumping carts. Ria signed something to him, eliciting a chuckle from Rohan.

Their hands met serendipitously in the bustling market, sparks igniting between them. With shy smiles, they both withdrew, a silent acknowledgment of the burgeoning connection.

In the kitchen, they cooked side by side, flour dusting their noses as they kneaded dough. Rohan patiently taught Ria, their faces close, their laughter filling the air.

Rohan became Ria's unwavering support, cheering her on from the stands as she competed at the city level. Her eyes sought out his reassuring presence, finding solace in his encouraging signs.

Guided by Rohan, Ria embraced meditation, her breaths steadying under his gentle guidance. She signed "Thank you," her expression serene, as she found inner peace.

Ria's training regimen intensified, encompassing physical and mental conditioning. She ran, lifted weights, and practiced archery with newfound determination and focus.

The Mysterious Woman , her face veiled in shadow, watched Ria and Rohan from a distance. Her fingers tightened on a pair of binoculars, her gaze lingering on Ria's smiling face with an intensity that bordered on obsession.

The Male Spirit watched over Ria, witnessing her transformation from a guarded individual to a woman embracing love and happiness.

The montage culminated with Ria receiving a letter. Her eyes widened in excitement as she read the contents, a grin spreading across her face. She excitedly signed to Rohan, "I made it! National level selection!" His face mirrored her joy, sharing in her triumph.

Determination burned in Ria's eyes as she prepared for her final match, where victory could propel her to the world stage of archery. The path ahead was fraught with challenges, but she wasn't alone.

She had Rohan, a beacon of hope and support, and the Male Spirit, a silent guardian, watching over her. The shadows that had threatened to consume her were fading, replaced by a glimmer of light, a promise of a future filled with love, passion, and the pursuit of her dreams.

CHAPTER TWENTY-FIVE

"The Shadow's Game"

Rohan found himself in a quaint chocolate shop, the air thick with the sweet aroma of cocoa and sugar. He browsed the shelves, his gaze flitting over rows of colorful chocolate bars, a hint of uncertainty clouding his features. He picked up a heart-shaped box, then set it down with a frown. Too cliché. His eyes landed on a bar of dark chocolate with sea salt, and he wrinkled his nose.

"Sea salt and chocolate?" he muttered to himself, a bewildered chuckle escaping his lips. "Who knew?"

He shrugged, a fond smile touching his lips, and added the unusual bar to his basket.

As he stepped out of the shop onto the busy street, the air thick with the sounds of city life, a black car screeched to a halt beside him. The doors flew open, and two masked men jumped out, their movements swift and brutal. One of them grabbed Rohan from behind, clamping a hand over his mouth, while the other pressed a chloroform-soaked cloth to his face.

Rohan struggled briefly, his eyes wide with panic, but the chloroform quickly took effect. He felt his body grow heavy, his senses fading, and then darkness enveloped him.

The tunnel was dim and dusty, illuminated by sparse rays of sunlight piercing through cracks in the crumbling ceiling. The air was thick with the smell of damp earth and decay. Rohan, his hands bound, stumbled as he was dragged roughly by two mercenaries through the oppressive darkness. He was disoriented, his head pounding, the lingering effects of the chloroform making him dizzy and confused.

As they reached the tunnel's midpoint, Rohan summoned a burst of strength and determination. He knew he had to fight back, to break free from this suffocating grip. With sudden ferocity, he propelled himself forward, head-butting one of the mercenaries with a force that sent him crashing to the ground.

Taking advantage of their momentary surprise, he freed his hands, his movements fueled by a surge of adrenaline. He delivered a powerful kick to the chest of the other assailant, sending him reeling backward. The mercenaries staggered and collapsed, writhing in agony on the dusty ground.

From the shadows, a third mercenary emerged, charging towards Rohan with deadly intent.Reacting swiftly, Rohan evaded the attack, executing a swift and precise maneuver that brought the assailant crashing to the ground. He swiftly overpowered the mercenary, pinning him down with a mixture of skill and desperation.

"Who sent you?" Rohan demanded, his voice furious. "Why did you kidnap me? Where is your boss? Tell me who's behind all of this!"

The mercenary's struggles intensified, his breaths labored and panicked. With trembling hands, he pointed frantically behind Rohan, towards the shadowy depths of the tunnel.

"What?" Rohan said, confused, skeptical. "There's no one there."

Rohan swiftly rendered the mercenary unconscious, then pivoted towards the direction the man had gestured. The atmosphere in the tunnel shifted, growing colder, sending a chill down his spine. A primal, guttural growl reverberated from the darkness, triggering an instinctual fear within him. He felt a sharp sting in his sinuses, and blood began to trickle from his nose.

"We've been waiting for you, V," a voice whispered from the darkness, a low, chilling voice that seemed to seep into his bones.

His blood ran cold. He turned towards the voice, his heart pounding. A hand instinctively reached for the locket at his neck, seeking comfort in its presence.

As Rohan recognized the familiar voice, a shiver of fear shot down his spine. His hand instinctively found the locket hanging around his neck, seeking comfort in its presence. Gripping it tightly, he felt a surge of energy coursing through him, causing his entire body to tremble. The air around him seemed to shimmer with an intense light, as if shaped by unseen forces. As the brilliance faded, Rohan disappeared, replaced by V, his expression a mixture of fury and confusion.

V turned, his movements deliberate, his eyes cutting through the darkness like a blade, anticipation palpable as he awaited the revelation of the speaker's identity.

From the shadows, Aira emerged with a confident stride, her features bathed in the dim light, accentuating the smug smirk playing on her lips.

V stared at Aira, his face a canvas of disbelief and dawning fury. Her smirk widened with satisfaction, casting a sinister shadow over her features. The air hung heavy with tension, the silence punctuated only by the drip-drip-drip of water from the tunnel's ceiling. The game had changed, the stakes raised. And the shadow that had haunted his life, that had threatened to consume him, had finally revealed itself.

CHAPTER TWENTY-SIX

"A FATHER'S SHADOW"

Flashback,Harsh sunlight sliced through the hospital room, illuminating the sterile white walls. A heart monitor beeped insistently, each sound a stark reminder of V's fragile state. He lay in bed, his face pale and gaunt, an oxygen mask muffling his labored breaths.

V stirred, confusion clouding his eyes as he ripped the mask away, gasping for air. Panic flooded his face as he yanked free the tubes in his arms, ignoring the stinging pain. He struggled to his feet, legs trembling, and stumbled towards the door.

The city noise assaulted him as he stumbled into the blinding sunlight. Car horns blared, sirens wailed, a dog barked. He clung to the wall, each step a fight against his weakening body. His legs buckled, and he collapsed onto the sidewalk.

A black car screeched to a halt. A silhouetted figure emerged, obscured by the harsh sunlight. V tried to scramble back, but strong arms lifted him effortlessly. His vision blurred, and darkness claimed him.

The car door slammed shut. Tires squealed as the car vanished into the city, leaving behind only the lingering echo of its presence.

V gasped awake, his chest heaving, a damp cloth falling from his forehead. His eyes darted around the room – his childhood home, every detail seared into his memory. The familiar scent of wood polish and baking bread, the worn rug beneath his feet, the faint hum of the refrigerator. He felt a sense of disorientation, a jarring contrast to the sterile white of the hospital room.

"How...?" he whispered, his voice hoarse, a question hanging in the air.

The door creaked open. His father entered, carrying a glass of water and a pill. His face, etched with a mixture of relief and shame, was one V had never seen before.

V tried to rise, anger flaring within him, but his legs failed him. His father caught him gently, his touch a stark contrast to the years of neglect.

"Careful, son," his father said, his voice laced with a tenderness V barely recognized.

"Son." The word pierced V. He stared at his father, a storm of emotions raging within him. Resentment, anger, confusion, a longing for the father he never had.

"Why now, Father?" he asked, his voice laced with bitterness. "After all these years...you act like you care?"

His father's face crumpled, his eyes filled with regret. "I was a coward, V. Your relatives...they threatened me. Hurt you, hurt Sylvie...I was afraid."

"Afraid?" V's voice rose, his anger simmering beneath the surface. "You were never there!"

"Not openly," his father said, his voice a low murmur. "But I watched over you. Arranged your rent house, paid your expenses...Even in the hospital..."

A flash of memory: Young V signing a lease, the kind landlord smiling. A blurry hand brushing V's forehead in a sterile hospital room.

Tears welled up in V's eyes, a torrent of emotions finally breaking through the dam of resentment. He rose, his body still weak, and embraced his father, a hug laden with years of unspoken pain, a yearning for the father he had always longed for.

"I'm sorry, Father," he whispered, the words a release, a letting go.

His father returned the embrace, tears in his eyes. He gently pulled back, wiping V's tears.

"It's alright, son. It's all alright. Now, wait here. I have something for you."

His father hurried upstairs, a newfound lightness in his step. V watched him go, then turned, a small, sad smile gracing his lips. The years of anger and resentment were fading, replaced by a flicker of hope, a yearning for the family he had lost.

Suddenly, the Female Spirit materialized before him, her form shimmering slightly, her expression a mixture of curiosity and amusement.

"So...peace reigns at last?" she asked, her voice a melodic whisper. "Ready to embrace dear old Dad?"

V looked at the Female Spirit, then back towards the stairs. A warmth spreading through him that had nothing to do with the sunlight streaming through the windows. He tilted his head, offering the spirit a genuine smile.

"Yes," he said softly. "Yes, I am."

The past had been a tumultuous journey, filled with pain, loss, and a profound sense of loneliness. But now, with the weight of the past lifted, V was ready to embrace a new future. The path ahead was uncertain, but he was no longer alone. He had a father, he had a spirit who had always watched over him, and he had a purpose. The pieces were falling into place, a new chapter about to begin.

CHAPTER TWENTY-SEVEN

"A DANCE OF SHADOWS"

V raised a hand, silencing both the Female Spirit and the insistent ringing of his phone. The caller ID: "Unknown Number."

"Don't move," he whispered to the spirit, his voice laced with urgency. "Don't say a word."

He took a deep breath and answered the call.

"Hello?"

Aiden leaned back in his leather chair, gazing out the floor-to-ceiling window at thesprawling cityscape below. He swirled a glass of amber liquid in his hand, a predatory smile playing on hislips. He enjoyed the game, the delicate dance of power and control.

"Ah, V," he said, his voice smooth and menacing. "It seems you've awoken from your little nap."

V's grip tightened on the phone. He felt a prickle of unease, a sense of foreboding. His initial relief at reconnecting with his father was fading, replaced by a growing sense of apprehension.

"Who is this?" he asked, his voice laced with caution. "How do you know me?"

Aiden took a slow sip of his drink, his eyes cold and calculating. He savored the moment, relishing the power he wielded.

"Let's just say I'm familiar with your...situation. And with the girl you love," Aiden said, his
voice dripping with malice.

V's blood ran cold. His mind raced, trying to piece together the connection, the threat. His heart hammered in his chest, the warmth of his reunion with his father replaced by a chilling fear.

"What are you talking about?" V demanded, his voice tight with apprehension.

Aiden let out a low chuckle, devoid of humor. He set down his glass, the sound echoing in the silent office.

"Let me be blunt," Aiden said, his voice a chilling whisper. "Stay away from her. Consider it a piece of friendly advice."

V's initial fear gave way to anger. He glanced up the stairs, ensuring his father was still out of earshot.

"So that's your game, is it?" he said, a humorless smile playing on his lips. "Want me out of the picture so you can hurt her?"

Aiden's expression turned to ice. He was no stranger to threats, to manipulation, to the dark arts of control.

"You're a fool if you think you can protect her, V," Aiden said, his voice laced with contempt. "This path you've chosen...it only leads to pain. For both of you."

V drew himself up, his voice hardening with resolve, but laced with raw emotion. "If you think you can hurt her, you'll have to go through me first," he said, his voice resonating with a newfound strength. "I don't care who you are, or what you think you know. I don't know what your motive is, why you're doing this..."

He paused, drawing a shaky breath, his voice gaining strength. The Female Spirit watched him, surprised by the depth of emotion she sensed in him. She had seen him struggle, seen his vulnerability, but now, she saw a man ready to fight for what he believed in.

"But I will find out," V continued, his voice unwavering. "And I will stop you."

Aiden's eyes narrowed. He leaned forward, his voice low and dangerous. "Brave words, V," he said, a hint of amusement in his tone. "But you need to be alive to save anyone. See, I know about you.

We're not so different, you and me. Both willing to sacrifice everything for the ones we love."

Fury flickered across V's face. He felt a surge of rage, a primal instinct to protect those he cared for. He couldn't allow this man to threaten Ria, to manipulate her life, to harm her in any way.

"But you," Aiden continued, his voice dripping with disdain, "you're afraid to get your hands dirty. Afraid of the cost. I'm not. I'll burn down the world to achieve my goal."

A chill raced down V's spine as he heard the unmistakable roar of engines outside – the same sound he heard before. He looked out the window and saw several cars pulling up, their windows tinted black. Men in dark suits emerged, their faces grim. The mercenaries. Aiden smiled, a cruel, predatory expression spreading across his face. "Let's see if your actions match your bravado, V," he said, his voice laced with malice. "Escape if you can. Prove to me you're more than just talk."

Aiden hung up the phone. The dial tone buzzed in V's ear like a venomous insect. V shoved the phone into his pocket, his heart pounding. He turned to the Female Spirit, his expression grim.

"We've got company," he said.

The Female Spirit descended from the ceiling, her form shimmering like heat haze.

"Impressive speech," she said, her voice laced with skepticism. "But you're outnumbered and outmatched. Leave this to me. I'll make sure they never even reach the door."

She started to drift towards the advancing mercenaries, but V stepped forward, his expression determined.

"Hold on," he said, his voice firm. "I'll handle this."

"Right," the Female Spirit scoffed. "And how do you plan to do that? Tell them to death?"

"It's a bet," V said, a mischievous glint in his eye. "I can take them down without laying a finger on them. And without my father suspecting a thing. Besides, if I can't even protect myself from them, how am I supposed to protect her? So yeah, I'm ready to face the challenge."

"No touching. No noise. No alarming Daddy Dearest," the Female Spirit said, intrigued.

"Interesting. You're on."

The Female Spirit ascended to the ceiling, settling on a rafter to get a better view. "Don't disappoint me," she said, her voice laced with amusement. "This had better be good."

The front door burst open, and the first wave of mercenaries charged in, their movements tense, professional. V stood his ground, a confident smile playing on his lips.

"Game on," he said.

The first mercenary, a hulking figure, burst through the doorway, followed by seven more, each a seasoned fighter. They fanned out, surrounding V. He stood calmly, his eyes scanning the room, committing every detail to memory. He knew this house, this space, like the back of his hand.

The Female Spirit, perched on the ceiling, shook her head, a smirk playing on her lips. "This should be entertaining," she muttered to herself.

The scene shifted into slow motion. A playful, yet tense score swelled, replacing the sounds of combat.

The Dance Begins

As the first two mercenaries charged, V stepped aside, simultaneously nudging a delicate antique side table just enough to disrupt their path. One mercenary tripped, crashing into his partner, setting off a domino effect as the others collided, creating a tangle of limbs and frustrated grunts. The air filled with the sounds of muffled crashes and startled cries.

V used his agility to weave through the remaining attackers, his movements fluid, almost invisible. He ducked under a wild punch, stepped aside as a kick whizzed past his head, using their momentum against them. He was a phantom, a ghost in their midst.

Spotting a grandfather clock with a swinging pendulum, V subtly shifted its weight, just enough to alter its rhythm. The mercenaries, focused on their target, didn't notice the change until it was too late. The pendulum, now swinging at head height, caught one off guard with a resounding CLUNK. He crumpled to the ground, his head spinning.

Two mercenaries cornered V near the grand staircase. He seemed trapped. But as one lunged, V stepped back, using the polished banister as a lever. The mercenary flew over the railing, landing with an undignified THUD on the plush carpet below. His partner, stunned by the sudden turn of events, hesitated, giving V the opening he needed to send him tumbling down the stairs with a well-placed foot.

The remaining mercenaries were closing in, their frustration mounting. V, breathing heavily but still untouched, saw his opportunity. He positioned himself strategically beneath a heavy chandelier, its crystals shimmering in the afternoon light. With a precise kick to a pressure-sensitive floorboard, he set the chandelier swaying. The mercenaries, blinded by its swinging light and confused by the sudden movement, collided with each other and the surrounding furniture in a cacophony of muffled crashes.

One by one, the mercenaries fell, victims of their own aggression and V's calculated chaos.

The Female Spirit watched with open admiration. She had never seen anything like it, this graceful, almost whimsical display of combat. She remembered this style somewhere, but the memory was hazy, elusive.

Suddenly, a wave of dizziness washed over her. She cried out, clutching her head. A vision, hazy but terrifying, flooded her senses: A face of men, his faces blurred, his eyes filled with a cold, calculating malice. She could feel the weight of their power, the threat they posed, but the vision was fragmented, unclear. The vision faded, leaving behind a residue of fear and unease.

Below, V surveyed the scene, his chest heaving, a thin sheen of sweat on his brow. The last mercenary crumpled to the floor, unconscious.

"Check and mate," V said, dusting his hands off.

Footsteps sounded on the stairs above. V's father was descending.

"Hide them!" V said urgently to the Female Spirit. "Now!"

The Female Spirit, still disoriented from her vision, waved a hand. The unconscious mercenaries vanished, instantly reappearing inside their vehicles outside. The engines roared to life, and the cars sped away.

V's father entered the hall, a framed photo in his hands. He frowned, looking around. "Was that...? Did I hear...? He looked at V, his eyes searching for an explanation.

V forced a casual smile. "Just the kids next door, Dad," he said, trying to sound nonchalant.

"They play a little rough sometimes."

His father seemed unconvinced, but he shrugged it off, handing V the photo. It was a picture of V's mother, her eyes crinkled in a warm smile.

"Come on, son," his father said. "Let's get some fresh air."

As they walked outside, the Female Spirit watched from the doorway, her expression troubled. The fight may be over, but something told her this was just the beginning. The shadows that had threatened them were still out there, their motives unclear, their intentions sinister. The game was far from over.

V and his father descended the steps of their home, a newfound ease settling between them.

The years of estrangement, the weight of unspoken words, seemed to lift, replaced by a tentative understanding, a shared desire for connection.

"I've got errands, V," his father said, a hint of hesitation in his voice. "Rest up, son."

He turned to leave, then paused, a thoughtful look on his face. "Actually...about your mother...her words about a 'noble gentleman'...I think you misunderstood."

V frowned, confusion clouding his features. "Misunderstood?"

His father's gaze softened with paternal love. "She didn't mean a job, V. Not a title. She meant something deeper. She wanted you to be a good man. Kind, brave...someone who stands up for what's right. That's the true mark of a noble man."

A flashback: The sterile white hospital room. Sylvie, frail but radiant, gazed at V with unwavering love, her eyes reflecting a profound wisdom.

V closed his eyes, remembering the weight of his mother's final words, the unspoken message she had conveyed.

"I understand, Father," he said softly. "I finally understand."

He looked at a photo of his mother, her eyes crinkled in a warm smile, her presence lingering in the air. He felt a surge of determination, a renewed sense of purpose.

"I'll honor her," he said, his voice resolute. "Not with a title, but with my character. Let me drive you for your errands."

His father smiled, a mixture of pride and relief washing over his face.

As V drove, the city blurring past the window, his father, in the passenger seat, pointed at a sleek car.

"Look at that, V," his father said. "New model. They say it practically drives itself."

V smiled, touched by his father's casual comment. He felt a sense of contentment, a fleeting moment of normalcy in the midst of the chaos that had consumed his life.

Suddenly, his father's face contorted in fear. "V! Look out!" he screamed.

A massive truck hurtled towards them, its horn blaring a desperate warning. There was no time to react, no time to avoid the inevitable.

CRUNCH! The impact threw the car sideways, flipping and spinning. The world became a blur of shattering glass, twisted metal, and blood.

V groaned, disoriented, hanging upside down. He saw his father, injured, slumped beside him.

"Father!" he gasped, his voice laced with fear and desperation.

He struggled with his jammed seatbelt, his body throbbing with pain.

"Hold on," he said, his voice strained. "I'm coming!"

He freed himself and helped his father upright. But his father cried out, his legs trapped.

"My leg..." he groaned.

Smoke billowed from the engine, the smell of burning metal filling the air. A terrifying sense of urgency gripped V.

"Don't worry," he said, trying to sound reassuring. "I'll get you out!"

But his father's eyes widened. He pointed towards the rear of the car. "V! Get out! It's going to explode!"

Flames licked at the undercarriage, the heat unbearable. V pulled his father, but the flames were spreading, the danger growing with each passing second.

In a desperate shove, his father sent V flying. "Go!" he screamed, his voice a mix of urgency and despair.

V landed hard on the pavement. He watched in horror as the car EXPLODED in a blinding flash, the sound of the explosion deafening. The air filled with the smell of burning rubber and metal.

Silence. The crackling of flames. V stared at the wreckage, his body battered, his heart shattered. He tried to speak, but only a primal scream erupted from his throat. His father's final words, his selfless act of sacrifice, echoed in his mind. "Go!"

He had lost his father, his connection to the past, the man who had finally offered him a flicker of hope. The world around him seemed to blur, his vision dimming. The weight of loss, the pain of betrayal, threatened to consume him.

He had been so close to mending the broken pieces of his life, to finding solace, to discovering a sense of belonging. But fate had dealt him a cruel hand, snatching away his father, leaving him alone once again. He was left with only the fragments of their reunion, the echoes of his father's words, a bittersweet reminder of what he had lost.

The shadows, once a symbol of his past, now loomed over him, a reminder of the darkness
that threatened to consume him. He had sworn to protect those he cared for, to fight for the ones he loved.

But now, he was alone, facing a world filled with darkness and uncertainty. And he had to find the strength
to continue.

CHAPTER TWENTY-EIGHT

"THE LOCKET'S PROMISE"

The main hall was a testament to the chaos that had just unfolded. Furniture lay overturned, fragments of broken glass glittered on the floor like fallen stars. V sat amidst the wreckage, his shoulders slumped, his face a mask of pain. He clenched and unclenched his fists, his whole body trembling with unshed tears and simmering rage.

He picked up a framed photograph, a younger, happier V, his face filled with youthful optimism. A strangled sob escaped his lips, and he hurled the picture across the room, the sound of it hitting the wall echoing through the silent house.

The Female Spirit materialized just in time, catching the frame before it shattered against the wall. She set it down gently on a nearby table, her brow furrowed with concern.

"V, stop this!" she said, her voice sharp with urgency. "What are you doing?"

V whirled around, his eyes blazing with a terrible light. "What does it look like?" he roared, his voice raw with pain. "I'm ANGRY! I should have been faster, stronger...I should have saved him!"

He slammed his fist against the wall, the sound echoing through the silent house.

"I'll kill him," he said, his voice a low growl. "I swear, I'll kill the bastard who did this!"

"Kill who?" the Female Spirit asked, her voice sharp, laced with urgency. "That man on the phone? Do you even know who he is? Where he is?"

V hesitated, his rage momentarily eclipsed by confusion. His mind was a whirlwind of emotions, his thoughts racing, trying to make sense of the chaos.

"Think, V!" the Female Spirit said, her voice softening. "What would your mother say if she saw you like this? Is this what she wanted for you? Consuming yourself with hatred and vengeance?"

V closed his eyes, his father's last words, his mother's dying wish, echoing in his ears. His shoulders slumped, the fight draining out of him, replaced by a wave of overwhelming despair.

"She wanted you to be better than this, V," the Female Spirit said, placing a hand on his shoulder, her touch gentle, her voice filled with empathy. "Braver. Stronger. She believed in you...believe in yourself."

"You can," she said, her voice encouraging. "You will. Remember what you told that man on the phone? You said you'd protect the ones you love."

V closed his eyes, recalling the conversation, the anger he felt, the fierce protectiveness that welled up inside him.

"What good are words when...?" he said, his voice trailing off.

He snapped his head up, his eyes wide with dawning realization. "Wait...did you say 'loved ones'?"

Without another word, he turned and raced out of the house, fear for the girl lending him a desperate speed.

(The Female Spirit watched him go, a mixture of worry and resignation on her face. She disappeared in a swirl of spectral energy, knowing she must follow.)

V ran through the dark streets, each stride fueled by adrenaline and a growing sense of dread.

He may not know her name, but he knew she was in danger. He couldn't let her face that danger alone.

(The focus is on V's determined face, illuminated by the streetlights as he races through the night. He's no longer driven by rage, but by a new purpose: to protect the girl who he loved, who had become entangled in a dangerous game.)

V peered through a window into Ria's bedroom. His breath caught in his throat. Ria lay asleep, her face pale, her hand bandaged, the white gauze stained with crimson. A wave of protectiveness, fierce and unwavering, washed over him.

He tried the doorknob. Locked. He pushed gently, then glanced around for another way in.

"You can't go in there," the Male Spirit said, appearing in a flicker of spectral light. "Stay back."

V jumped back, startled. He stared at the Male Spirit, his eyes wide with surprise. "Another spirit? But...you're..."

He stopped, shaking his head. Right now, the how and why of their spectral existence was irrelevant.

"Never mind," he said. "Listen, I need to help her! Her hand...what happened? Was it those men?"

"I'll explain," the Male Spirit said, his voice laced with worry. "But first, tell me...why do you care so much? What is she to you?"

V hesitated, at a loss for words. How could he explain the depth of his feelings, the instant connection he felt, to someone he barely knew?

"What do you know about her?" the Male Spirit asked, his voice a gentle probe. "Her dreams, her fears, her pain? Why does her safety matter so much to you?"

The Male Spirit raised a hand, spectral energy gathering at his fingertips. He unleashed a wave of power, a swirling vortex of blue light that engulfed V. Images flashed through V's mind: Ria laughing with her parents, her face lit up with joy; Ria struggling to master a difficult archery technique, her determination etched on her face; Ria crying silently in the darkness after the betrayal and her mistreated teacher event, her shoulders shaking with unshed tears. He saw her strength, her vulnerability, her loneliness... and her pain. He saw the little girl he had met years ago, the half-locket he had given her, and the years of unspoken connection that had bound them.

The vision faded, leaving V reeling, his heart aching with empathy. He understood now, on a level deeper than words, the woman she was, the life she'd lived. He had glimpsed a piece of her soul, and it resonated with his own.

V blinked, tears welling up in his eyes – not tears of sorrow this time, but of recognition, of bittersweet joy. He looked at Ria, a new understanding dawning in his eyes.

"So it was her," he said, his voice a soft whisper. "That little girl...all those years ago..."

He touched his chest, remembering the weight of the half-locket, a tangible link to a shared past.

"Yes, V," the Male Spirit said, nodding slowly. "She was the one. And she still wears your locket...a reminder of the boy who saved her."

V's face broke into a genuine smile, his heart lighter than it's been all day. He looked at Ria, a newfound hope blossoming within him. She wasn't just the woman he saw in glimpses and visions, not just a stranger in need of protection. She was a part of his past, a girl he had helped, a girl who, unknowingly, had carried a piece of his heart for all these years.

But the danger was far from over. V remembered the urgency of the situation.

"Listen," he said, his voice laced with determination. "We need to act fast. And there's something you can do to help."

"What is it?" the Male Spirit asked, hope flickering in his voice. "Anything."

"Use your power," V said. "Heal her hand. She needs to be strong, needs to fight for her dreams. She's carried so much on her own. So much pain. I...I can't let her face this alone."

"I want to protect her too," the Male Spirit said, his voice softening. "But...I'm bound to this place. And those men...they won't stop."

V thought quickly, his mind racing. "I have an idea," he said. "I'll stay with her. Protect her.Be her...support."

"But...how?" the Male Spirit asked, confused. "She doesn't know you. And she doesn't trust you."

"Not as V," V said, meeting the Male Spirit's gaze, his voice low and intense. "As...Rohan."

The Male Spirit stared at him, bewildered. "As...Rohan? Are you serious? Do you really think that will work? She's not a fool, V."

"I don't know if it will work," V said, his voice filled with a desperate hope. "But I have to try. Her safety...it's more important than anything, even my own identity. You asked me why I care so much..."

He paused, drawing in a shaky breath, his voice thick with unspoken emotion. "Because I love her. Even if she never feels the same, even if she hates me for it...I can live with that. But I can't live with myself if something happens to her, and I didn't do everything in my power to stop it. I know I don't have time left to live...but I will protect her even at my last minute of death."

He looked towards Ria's door, his eyes filled with a desperate hope.

(From the shadows, the Female Spirit watched him, her expression unreadable. She's seen centuries of love and loss, of promises made and broken. But there's something about V's unwavering determination that gives her pause.)

"Help me protect her," V said, his voice a plea. "Please."

The Male Spirit hesitated, then nodded slowly. "Then let's do this," he said, a flicker of hope in his voice. "For Ria."

V turned and walked towards the front door, pausing at the threshold to cast one last glance towards the room where Ria slept, oblivious to the danger she's in...and the lengths to which he's willing to go to keep her safe.

CHAPTER TWENTY-NINE

"THE PRICE OF A LIE"

The main hall was shrouded in shadows, the overturned furniture and scattered fragments of broken glass a grim reminder of the chaos that had just unfolded. V paced restlessly, his shoulders slumped, his face a canvas of raw emotion. He clenched and unclenched his fists, his whole body trembling with unshed tears and simmering rage.

He picked up a framed photograph – a younger, happier V, his face filled with youthful optimism. He clutched it tightly, the image of his past self a painful reminder of the life he had lost. A strangled sob escaped his lips, and he hurled the picture across the room.

The Female Spirit materialized just in time, catching the frame before it shattered against the wall. She set it down gently on a nearby table, her brow furrowed with concern.

"V, stop this!" she said, her voice sharp with urgency. "What are you doing?"

V whirled around, his eyes blazing with a terrible light. "What does it look like?" he roared, his voice raw with pain. "I'm ANGRY! I should have been faster, stronger...I should have saved him!"

He slammed his fist against the wall, the sound echoing through the silent house.

"I'll kill him," he said, his voice a low growl. "I swear, I'll kill the bastard who did this!"

"Kill who?" the Female Spirit asked, her voice sharp, laced with urgency. "That man on the phone? Do you even know who he is?

Where he is?"

V hesitated, his rage momentarily eclipsed by confusion. His mind was a whirlwind of emotions, his thoughts racing, trying to make sense of the chaos.

"Think, V!" the Female Spirit said, her voice softening. "What would your mother say if she saw you like this? Is this what she wanted for you? Consuming yourself with hatred and vengeance?"

V closed his eyes, his father's last words, his mother's dying wish, echoing in his ears. His shoulders slumped, the fight draining out of him, replaced by a wave of overwhelming despair.

"She wanted you to be better than this, V," the Female Spirit said, placing a hand on his shoulder, her touch gentle, her voice filled with empathy. "Braver. Stronger. She believed in you...believe in yourself."

"You can," she said, her voice encouraging. "You will. Remember what you told that man on the phone? You said you'd protect the ones you love."

V closed his eyes, recalling the conversation, the anger he felt, the fierce protectiveness that welled up inside him.

"What good are words when...?" he said, his voice trailing off.

He snapped his head up, his eyes wide with dawning realization. "Wait...did you say 'loved ones'?"

Without another word, he turned and raced out of the house, fear for the girl lending him a desperate speed.

The Female Spirit watched him go, a mixture of worry and resignation on her face. She disappeared in a swirl of spectral energy, knowing she must follow, her presence a silent guardian.

V ran through the dark streets, each stride fueled by adrenaline and a growing sense of dread.

He may not know her name, but he knew she was in danger. He couldn't let her face that danger alone.

The Female Spirit observed V as he paced restlessly, his movements agitated, his face a mask of conflicting emotions. "So, you're willing to become someone else entirely?" she asked, her voice a soft whisper. "To live a lie, even if it means she may never know the truth of your sacrifice?"

V stopped pacing, his expression resolute. "Yes," he said, his voice firm. "My feelings, my identity...those are insignificant compared to her safety. But...I don't even know where to start. How can I possibly become someone else?"

The Female Spirit stared at him, her usual playful demeanor replaced by a surprising tenderness. V's selfless determination had shifted something within her, stirring a well of empathy she thought long dormant.

"Perhaps...I can help with that," she said, her voice softer than usual.

V stopped pacing, his head snapping up, eyes widening in surprise. He stared at the Female Spirit, speechless for a moment.

"You...you would do that?" he asked, a glimmer of hope sparking in his eyes. "For me?"

The Female Spirit hesitated, a flicker of something unreadable in her eyes. "Don't get any ideas," she said, her voice regaining its usual playful tone. "This doesn't mean I approve. But...you intrigue me, V. You and your reckless heart."

She raised her hand, spectral energy swirling around her fingers. V watched, a mixture of apprehension and hope swirling within him.

The air crackled with energy, a blue light emanating from the Female Spirit. V stood unmoving, his gaze fixed on hers as the light engulfed him.

The light faded. V looked down at his hands, flexing his fingers. They looked...different.

Stronger. He rushed towards a nearby mirror, staring at his reflection in disbelief. Gone was the familiar face he'd known his entire life. Staring back at him was...Rohan. His features, his build, even his clothes had been flawlessly replicated down to the smallest detail.

"I...I look..." he said, his voice no longer his own. It was Rohan's – deeper, more confident.

He touched his face, a shiver running down his spine. It was both exhilarating and terrifying.

"Thank you," he said, turning back to the Female Spirit, his voice filled with gratitude. "I don't know how I can ever repay you..."

As he spoke, the Female Spirit swayed, her form flickering, her power waning. V caught her, concern etched on his features.

"Are you alright?" he asked, his voice laced with worry. "What's wrong?"

"It's...the transformation," she said, her voice weak. "It took more out of me than I anticipated. I...I need to recover. Also, remember, this power will protect you from your blood cancer as well. It will slow down the cause."

She steadied herself, drawing in a deep, shuddering breath. "But V...before you go...remember what you're sacrificing. What if she never knows the truth? What will you do then?"

V hesitated, a flicker of pain crossing his face. It was a question he hadn't allowed himself to fully confront. The consequences, the potential for heartbreak, loomed large.

"Then that's a burden I'll bear," he said, a sad smile touching his lips. "Her happiness is worth more than my pride."

He touched the heart-shaped locket at his throat, a tangible reminder of the connection he shared with Ria, a connection that started in childhood innocence and has now led him down this extraordinary, perilous path.

"And when all of this is over?" the Female Spirit asked, her voice laced with a touch of wonder. "When she's achieved her dreams and this...Aiden...is no longer a threat...what then?"

V's gaze hardened with resolve. "Then I'll step aside," he said, his voice unwavering. "She deserves to be happy. With or without me. But until then...I'll be her shield. Her Rohan."

The Female Spirit stared at him, her expression unreadable. For a being who existed outside of time, V's capacity for love, for sacrifice, was a mystery she was only just beginning to unravel.

"So how do you plan on approaching her?" she asked after a beat of silence. "She's wary of strangers, especially after the attack."

V smirked, a glint of mischief in his eyes. He had a plan, a risky one, but one he was willing to gamble on. He had to trust his instincts, his intuition, and his heart.

The montage unfolded, a tapestry woven from stolen moments and unspoken feelings. V, alone in his room, clutched the heart-shaped locket, its cool metal a constant reminder of his connection to Ria. He could almost feel her presence, her spirit intertwined with his. A single tear rolled down his cheek as he whispered, "For you, Ria. Always for you."

He had taken a leap of faith, transforming himself into Rohan, a seemingly ordinary man, to protect Ria. He orchestrated a series of chance encounters, each one carefully planned, each one designed to draw her closer.

He had rescued her from a group of men who had harassed her on a dark street, his movements swift and decisive. As he walked her home, he saw a flicker of respect in her eyes, a hint of something more that made his heart flutter.

He had anonymously sent her a photograph, capturing her in a moment of perfect concentration during her archery practice. Beneath the picture, a single line: "You are a warrior." The words resonated with her, reminding her of her strength and potential.

He had bumped into her at a local cafe, their hands brushing as they both reached for a fallen book. Their eyes met for a moment, a silent spark igniting between them. He saw a vulnerability beneath her guarded exterior, a vulnerability that tugged at his heart.

They had raced through the city on his motorcycle, the wind whipping through their hair, the city lights blurring into a dazzling kaleidoscope. They had ended up at a secluded spot overlooking the cityscape, sharing stolen moments of laughter and connection.

V's heart ached with a longing for Ria. He watched her laugh, his heart swelling with a bittersweet joy, a love he could only express in stolen glances, in whispered words. He saw her as a warrior, as a survivor, as a woman who had overcome so much.

He had gently guided her through a throng of reporters after her archery tournament victory, a silent protector, a comforting presence. As the photographers called for a picture, he whispered, "This is your moment," and stepped back, melting into the crowd.

For a fleeting second, as he turned away from her, he was V again, his expression filled with a painful tenderness. Then, he was Rohan once more, rejoining Ria, his smile genuine despite the ache in his heart.

He sat at his desk, exhaustion etched on his face as he stared at a pile of govt exam books.

He had poured his heart into supporting Ria, into being her Rohan, while neglecting his own ambitions. Just as he was about to close a book in defeat, the doorbell rang. He went outside and found a gift on his

doorstep.

Intrigued, he tore it open. Inside, nestled amongst protective packaging, lay a brand-new set of govt study guides. His heart leaped as he spotted a handwritten note tucked inside: "Best of luck, V. Try your best. I'm looking forward to seeing you clear this exam. With hearty congrats (heart emoji). P.S. Best of luck for your final exam and final attempt."

V searched for a sender's name, but the note was unsigned. Confusion washed over him, quickly followed by a surge of warmth as he reread the message. He felt a surge of determination. He would clear this exam, for himself, for his father...and for this mysterious well-wisher.

Days turned into weeks, weeks into months. V poured himself into his studies, pushing himself to his limits. He also continued to support Ria, cheering her on as she trained, celebrated her victories, and faced new challenges.

He checked the govt first exam results online, his heart pounding. He had passed! The joy was short-lived as he realized the next hurdle – the mains exam – loomed large.

He celebrated with Ria as she was selected for the national archery championship. He was proud of her, truly happy for her, but a part of him ached with the knowledge that her success would bring their time together to an end.

He sat at his desk, exhaustion and anticipation etched on his face as he awaited the results of the mains exam. He had given everything he had to both parts of his life, to honoring his promise to the girl and to pursuing his own dreams. But now, fate hung in the balance.

The montage faded, the image of V, his face illuminated by the screen, his expression a mixture of hope and uncertainty. His journey was far from over, but he was determined to keep his promise to Ria, to protect her, to be her Rohan, even if it meant sacrificing everything he held dear.

CHAPTER THIRTY

"A BIRTHDAY REVELATION"

Sunlight spilled across the worn floorboards of Ria's living room, bathing the space in a warm glow. Ria, a whirlwind of excited gestures, ushered Rohan towards the front door. Her hands flew, signing rapid-fire:

"Chocolate. Shop. Now! Sea salt. Remember?"

Rohan chuckled, used to her silent demands. "Yeah, yeah, I remember," he signed back. "Sea salt. You and your fancy chocolate. What's the special occasion?"

Ria rolled her eyes playfully, a mischievous glint in them. She signed back, her expression a mixture of affection and mock exasperation.

"Go! Just go!"

She gave him a gentle push towards the door, her smile widening as he shook his head fondly and stepped outside. The moment the door clicked shut, the playful mask melted away. Ria rushed to her bedroom, a quiet urgency in her movements.

The afternoon sun cast the room in a warm glow. She pulled open a drawer, her fingers hovering over a rectangular cardboard box before gently lifting it out.

The box was placed carefully on the bed, its lid opened to reveal a beautiful chocolate cake, decorated with swirls of frosting. On top, in elegant script, sat the words: "HAPPY BIRTHDAY DEAR V."

A soft gasp escaped Ria's lips. Her eyes welled up, reflecting the unspoken emotions swirling within her. She glanced towards the window, searching for any sign of Rohan's return.

Her hand reached for a locket nestled beneath her collarbone. It was a heart-shaped locket, and she clutched it tightly, tracing its contours with a trembling thumb. A watery smile touched her lips as she caught her reflection in the mirror, her eyes shining with love and a hint of melancholy.

A flashback:

The image of Ria's reflection in the bathroom mirror dissolved into a close-up of her face, now streaked with water, staring at her own troubled eyes. Her gaze shifted to the calendar hanging on the wall. The date circled in bright red jumped out at her: tomorrow, her birthday.

A shadow passed over Ria's face. The joylessness of the day, the heavy weight of the anniversary of her parents' death, hung in the air like a shroud. With a sudden, violent gesture, she crumpled the calendar in her fist, tossing it into the nearby trash bin.

Moving with a determined stride, she entered the training area, a place of familiar solace and focus. She nocked an arrow, drew back the string of her bow, her movements precise and controlled. The arrow flew, a silver streak aimed at the heart of the target.

But just before it hit, a figure materialized in front of the target – a female spirit, ethereal and otherworldly, catching the arrow inches from her chest.

Ria froze, a gasp escaping her lips. Shock gave way to a steely resolve as she recognized the danger emanating from the spectral figure. This was no ordinary woman. This was something...else.

Ria didn't hesitate. She grabbed another arrow, her movements a blur as she fired a volley of shots at the spectral female spirit. The female spirit moved with an unnerving grace, deflecting each arrow with a flick of her wrist, the air shimmering around her with each deflected projectile.

The room became a whirlwind of motion and light. Ria's arrows were met with the female spirit's uncanny ability to manipulate their trajectory, bending them to her will. One arrow, aimed for the female spirit's heart, spun mid-air, turning back towards Ria with unnatural speed.

Just as it was about to strike her, the female spirit raised her hand. A wave of energy burst from her palm, engulfing the arrow and stopping it inches from Ria's chest. But the energy didn't dissipate.

It surged forward, a torrent of light that crashed into Ria, surrounding her, searing her with visions.

Images flashed before her eyes. A young boy, his face etched with pain and loneliness. ASylvie, her voice filled with love and a promise she couldn't keep.

And then, amidst the chaos of images, a moment of clarity. The boy, his face illuminated by the warm glow of a streetlamp, holding out a heart-shaped locket. It was the same locket Ria wore around her neck. It was V.

More images flooded her mind. V, through the years, his silent sacrifices for her, the careful web he'd woven to keep her safe, culminating in his transformation into Rohan.

The vision faded, leaving Ria breathless and reeling. The energy dissipated, leaving her standing there, bow slack in her hand, tears streaming down her face.

She looked at the female spirit, her expression a mixture of awe and dawning understanding.

The female spirit's lips moved, the words forming soundlessly, reaching Ria's ears as if from a great distance.

Ria understood, reading her lips, the truth of V's sacrifice.

"He was ready to sacrifice his happiness for yours," the female spirit said. "He didn't expect anything in return, only your safety. But perhaps...perhaps he hoped for your love."

Ria's hands trembled as she signed back, her voice thick with tears and remorse.

"I feel so guilty...so ashamed," she signed. "I didn't understand...his love, his intentions...but I do now. I want to tell him...show him..."

"Then do it," the female spirit said, a faint smile playing on her lips. "On his birthday. After your final match."

Confusion clouded Ria's features. "But...why?" she signed. "Why not now?"

"Have you forgotten?" the female spirit said, her voice a soft whisper. "You met him for the first time in the park...on his birthday."

Ria stared at the Female Spirit, stunned. It all fell into place. The timing, the significance of the date, the unspoken connection. She had been oblivious, lost in her own grief, but now, the truth was revealed, a revelation that brought a surge of hope and a wave of longing.

"And...don't tell him that I know the truth about him," she signed, her voice laced with a new determination. "About V."

The female spirit nodded, a faint smile playing on her lips, before dissolving into thin air. Ria stood alone in the training room, the weight of the truth settling upon her like a physical burden. But it wasn't a burden of sorrow. It was a burden of love. And a fierce determination to finally, truly, see the man who had loved her from the shadows.

The flashback faded, leaving Ria with a heart filled with a bittersweet longing, a longing for the man who had become her Rohan. She was ready to meet him, to face him, to tell him the truth. And she was ready to let him know that she loved him, a love that had bloomed in the face of adversity, a love that had survived the darkness.

CHAPTER THIRTY-ONE

"The Match of Fury"

The last rays of the setting sun painted the room in a warm glow, casting long shadows across the floorboards. Ria stood before her mirror, a soft smile gracing her lips as she adjusted a stray strand of hair. She had carefully arranged a plate of chocolate squares on the coffee table – V's favorite. She was about to send him a message, a simple "Happy Birthday," but she hesitated. What else could she say?

How could she express the whirlwind of emotions swirling within her?

Suddenly, a figure shimmered into existence beside her. It was the Male Spirit, his presence radiating a gentle warmth.

"So, the truth is out, is it?" he said, a playful smirk on his face.

Ria turned, her smile widening as she signed, "You could say that."

The Male Spirit chuckled, his expression turning serious. "Tell me, Ria," he said, his voice laced with a hint of concern. "When you look at him...who do you see? Rohan...or V?"

The question hung in the air, heavy with unspoken meaning. Ria's smile faltered for a moment before she gently took the Male Spirit's hand in hers, placing it over her heart. Her eyes, shimmering with unshed tears, met his gaze.

"His appearance may be Rohan's, but it's V's heart that beats within him," she signed with quiet conviction. "It's V's soul I see, his kindness, his strength...It's V I love."

The Male Spirit was silent for a moment, his eyes filled with a mixture of emotions. "At last," he whispered, his voice choked with emotion, "they understand each other."

Ria, lost in her own thoughts, didn't notice his reaction. She turned back towards the mirror, her gaze falling on the locket hanging around her neck. She touched it gently, her fingers tracing the familiar shape, her heart overflowing with a love that had only deepened with time.

A Montage of Flashback

Fireworks of Love: It was Ria's birthday. We saw her from behind, her back to as she stared up at the night sky in wonder. Fireworks erupted above her, forming a dazzling display of light and color. It was a scene ripped straight out of her archery dreams, each fiery arrow finding its mark in the night sky.

Behind her, V, as Rohan, watched her reaction with a mixture of hope and trepidation.

Ria's face broke into a radiant smile as she turned, about to face Rohan, but her expression quickly shifted to one of feigned surprise, masking the depth of her emotions. She knew the truth, but she was playing along, relishing the shared joy of the moment, savoring the connection they were building.

Dreams Rekindled: Ria stood in a bookstore, her eyes scanning the shelves until they landed on a stack of govt exam preparation books. Her gaze softened as she remembered V's dream – to become a government officer. His ambition, his longing for a better future, resonated with her.

Later, we saw her sneaking into Rohan's home, placing the gift-wrapped books on his doorstep. She hid outside, watching from a distance as he discovered her present. A proud smile touched her lips as she observed him, day after day, pouring over the books, his determination fueled by her silent love and support. She wanted him to achieve his dreams, to find the happiness he deserved.

The montage ended.

Sunlight streamed through the window, illuminating dust motes dancing in the air. Ria, athletic and determined, paced restlessly, her archery equipment bag slung over her shoulder.

"Ria, it's time," the Male Spirit said. "Your final national selection event. Remember what's on the line?"

Ria ran a hand through her hair, her movements jerky, her anxiety evident.

"One of you will be chosen for the international team," the Male Spirit said. "The other..."

Ria glanced at the door, anxiety etched on her face. She was looking for V, hoping he would arrive, hoping he would be there to support her.

"Don't tell me those nerves are getting to you now," the Male Spirit said, his voice laced with amusement. "Not after all this work."

Ria took a deep breath, trying to appear calm, and headed out.

The archery stadium hummed with anticipation. Spectators found their seats, their excited chatter echoing through the open structure. Ria stood alone, a rigid silhouette against the vast blue sky. She methodically checked her equipment, her movements precise, almost robotic. She was focused, determined, but a sense of unease lingered, a weight she couldn't shake off.

She pulled out a familiar arrow, its fletching worn smooth from practice. A small inscription caught the light – "For your strength, Abi." A ghost of a smile flickered across Ria's face. She remembered her mentor, his encouragement, his unwavering belief in her.

A hush fell over the crowd. Ria's eyes darted nervously towards the entrance. A sleek car pulled up, its windows tinted black. This was it.

Raju, the manager, emerged first. He scanned the crowd with a predatory gaze, his smile failing to reach his cold eyes. Ria's hand tightened around her bow. She remembered his words, his chilling motivation.

"My boss needs this championship," he had said. "You understand?"

Then, Aira stepped out of the car.

Ria's breath caught in her throat. Her friend, her teammate, looked effortlessly confident in her competition attire. But her eyes were cold, distant, devoid of the warmth that once marked their friendship.

A wave of betrayal washed over Ria. She remembered their encounter, the hidden truth revealed, the unspoken threat.

Aira caught Ria's eye but quickly looked away, a muscle ticking in her jaw. She ignored Ria's attempt at a small wave, her face an emotionless mask.

The announcer's voice boomed through the stadium, announcing the finalists. Ria took her position, her face a storm of conflicting emotions – anger, betrayal, but beneath it all, a flicker of steely determination.

The atmosphere crackled with the electricity of a high-stakes competition. The rhythmic twang of bowstrings punctuated the expectant silence of the crowd.

"Welcome back to the National Archery Selection Finals!" the announcer's voice boomed through the stadium speakers. "We're entering the second round of an incredible match between two of our country's finest young archers - Aira and Ria!"

On the screen, the scores were displayed: Aira - 10, Ria - 9.

Aira, a picture of cool confidence, stepped up to the line. Her movements were precise, almost mechanical in their efficiency. The arrow flew true, landing cleanly in the center ring.

"Another solid shot from Aira!" the announcer said. "She makes it look effortless!"

Across the arena, Ria felt a knot of tension tightening in her stomach. Her hand unconsciously moved to the locket nestled beneath her competition jersey – a constant reminder of her hidden struggle, of the sacrifices V had made for her.

On the sidelines, unseen, the Male Spirit and Female Spirit observed the unfolding drama, their ethereal forms a silent presence.

"She's not herself," the Male Spirit said. "That encounter with Aira is weighing on her."

"The pressure is immense," the Female Spirit said. "To think she's carrying that burden, both physically and emotionally..."

Ria stepped up to the line, drawing in a deep, steadying breath. She raised her bow, attempting to find her usual rhythm, but something felt off. The familiar weight of the weapon felt heavier, the string more resistant. The pain in her hand, a constant reminder of her injury, was exacerbated by the emotional turmoil she was facing.

"Ria seems a little out of sorts this round," the announcer said. "Will she be able to pull it together? This is her moment to answer Aira's challenge!"

With a shaky exhale, Ria released the arrow. It hit the target, but not with her usual precision.

Not even close to the center.

The score changed: Aira - 20, Ria – 18. Frustration flickered across Ria's face.

A FEW ROUNDS LATER.

"And we're into the fourth round of our national selection final!" the announcer's voice boomed through the stadium speakers. "The tension is palpable here as Aira maintains her narrow lead. Can Ria pull back in these final rounds?"

A digital scoreboard blazed above the finalists: Aira - 39, Ria - 36.

A hush descended as Aira stepped up, her face impassive. She drew the bowstring back, her movements a study in controlled power. The arrow flew, piercing the target just outside the bullseye.

"Another excellent shot from Aira!" the announcer said. "The pressure is mounting on Ria."

Ria bit her lip, her hand unconsciously moving to the locket around her neck. She could practically feel V's worried gaze on her from the stands. She had told him that she was going to be okay, that she could handle this, but the truth was, she was struggling.

On the sidelines, unseen, the Male Spirit and Female Spirit watched intently.

"She seems off," the Female Spirit said. "Her timing is all wrong."

"That confrontation with Aira shook her," the Male Spirit said. "She's fighting more than just her opponent now. She's fighting her own demons."

Ria took her position, trying to block out everything but the target. She raised the bow, her movements less fluid than usual, but still precise. She focused on her breath, trying to regain her composure.

"Can Ria regain her composure?" the announcer asked. "This could be a crucial moment in the match!"

She released the arrow. It hit the target, but not as cleanly as she'd hoped.

The score changed: Aira - 42, Ria - 39.

Ria closed her eyes, took a breath. This was it. She had to fight back. She had to find her strength.

"Here it comes," the Male Spirit said, his voice a low whisper.

"What? What is she doing?" the Female Spirit asked, her voice filled with concern.

Ria reached up and unclasped her locket. She carefully put the locket into her pocket.

"She's chosen," the Male Spirit said, a hint of admiration in his voice. "She's going to face this her own way."

"But her hands...how can she possibly shoot without...?" the Female Spirit asked, bewildered.

The Male Spirit turned to her, his expression serious.

"Because sometimes, the pain inside is far worse than any physical injury," he said. "Seeing her closest friend become her enemy...that betrayal cuts deep. She's hurting, but not just physically. For Ria, that pain in her hands is nothing compared to what she feels inside."

The Female Spirit fell silent, her gaze drawn back to Ria. The young archer's face was a mixture of agony and fierce determination.

"Watch her," the Male Spirit said. "This is where her true strength will be tested."

Both spirits turned back to the arena, their eyes fixed on Ria's every move as she prepared to shoot.

The focused on Ria's face, a tapestry of pain and fierce determination. Her fingers, now trembling, struggled to grip the bow. Each movement sent a jolt of agony through her. But she wouldn't give up. She wouldn't let the pain, the betrayal, the fear, break her.

V flinched from the audience, as if sharing in her pain. He could only watch helplessly, his heart aching for her.

The rounds continued.

Despite her disadvantage, a new fire seemed to burn in Ria. She fought through the pain, each arrow a testament to her willpower. The scoreboard now read: Aira - 48, Ria - 48.

The final arrows of the special arrow given by her mentor, Abi.

Aira shot first. The arrow hit dead center. A bullseye. The stadium erupted in a wave of applause.

All eyes turned to Ria.

She took her position, her body shaking with exertion. The bow trembled in her grasp. The pain was almost unbearable, but she forced herself to focus. She drew the bowstring back, her gaze unwavering, locked on the target.

For a moment, everything was still.

Then, with a shuddering breath, she released.

Time seemed to slow. The arrow arced through the air, a silver thread against the blue sky. It spun, carrying with it all her pain, her frustration, her burning desire to overcome. And it found its mark.

Bullseye.

Ria collapsed to her knees, the bow clattering to the ground beside her. A wave of dizziness washed over her, but through the haze, she saw it: V, jumping to his feet, a roar of victory escaping his lips.

She heard her own victory cry, a sound that echoed through the stadium.

Golden light, the last gasp of day, painted long shadows across the nearly deserted parking lot.

Aira, small and slight, practically sprinted backward across the asphalt, her sneakers squeaking desperately. Her head whipped back and forth, eyes wide with fear – a trapped animal. Her beat-up hatchback, the only escape route, sat tantalizingly close.

A hand shot out, catching Aira's arm in a vice-like grip. A sharp cry escaped Aira's lips as she was spun around, momentum carrying them both to the ground in a tangle of limbs.

Ria, face contorted with fury, pinned Aira to the asphalt. Their struggle was a whirlwind of flailing arms and legs, grunts of exertion replacing words.

Aira's eyes, wide with panic, darted between Ria's face and the hatchback, now just out of reach.

The keys, ripped from Aira's grasp, skittered across the pavement, landing with a clatter somewhere behind them.

For a heartbeat, they were frozen, Aira trapped beneath Ria's weight, chests heaving.

Then, with a victorious roar, Ria threw Aira aside, scrambling to her knees, hand outstretched towards the fallen figure.

But Aira was already moving. While Ria savored her momentary triumph, Aira scrambled toward the hatchback, scrambling inside. The car door slammed shut between them.

Through the windshield, Ria saw Aira's panicked scramble for the keys, the engine sputtering, then roaring to life. The car lurched backward.

Ria lunged, her fingers grasping only air as the hatchback sped away, leaving her kneeling alone on the asphalt.

Her eyes fell on something glinting on the ground where she landed – Aira's pistol, forgotten in the struggle.

Ria picked it up. Her face, a mask of fury, hardened with resolve.

She sprinted towards her own car.

CHAPTER THIRTY-TWO

"THE BRIDGE OF FATE"

Ria threw open the car door, leaped in, and slammed it shut. The engine roared, a mechanical echo of her fury. She slammed the car into gear and roared out of the parking lot, tires spitting gravel.

Behind her, V skidded to a stop, taking in the scene: Aira's abandoned hatchback, the skid marks, and the empty space where Ria's car had been just moments ago. His eyes widened with alarm as he spotted the glint of metal on the ground – Aira's dropped pistol. He understood instantly.

With a curse, V raced towards his motorcycle, parked nearby. He had to follow her, to protect her, to ensure she wouldn't make a rash decision, a decision fueled by anger and grief.

Fat raindrops began to fall as Aira's hatchback tore through the city streets. She pushed the car to its limits, weaving through traffic, the rhythmic swish-swish of the windshield wipers barely keeping up with the downpour.

Behind her, headlights appeared, growing rapidly closer. Aira risked a glance in the rearview mirror – Ria, her face illuminated by the headlights, was a study in cold fury. Terror lent Aira speed.

Fat raindrops began to fall as Aira's hatchback tore through the city streets. She pushed the car to its limits, weaving through traffic, the rhythmic swish-swish of the windshield wipers barely keeping up with the downpour. The city lights blurred into a dizzying kaleidoscope of reflected neon, shimmering in the flooded streets. She could feel Ria's rage, a tangible force, hot on her heels.

Behind her, headlights appeared, growing rapidly closer. Aira risked a glance in the rearview mirror – Ria, her face illuminated by the headlights, was a study in cold fury. Terror lent Aira speed.

The downpour intensified, the rain a blinding curtain. The wind howled, buffeting the cars as they sped through the city, a symphony of sound and motion.

Ria, now perilously close, leaned out the window, ignoring the danger, her face a grimace of pain. The gun gleamed in her hand, its weight heavy, a constant reminder of her injured hand. She aimed, her focus laser-sharp.

A loud BANG echoed over the water.

Aira's car skidded violently, the rear end fishtailing as a tire blew. She fought for control, the car spinning precariously close to the bridge's edge.

V, on his motorcycle, roared through the rain, his engine a desperate howl. He weaved through traffic, adrenaline coursing through his veins. He saw Aira's car spinning out of control, saw Ria's determination, saw the approaching ambulance in the distance.

The bridge was a ribbon of asphalt stretching over a dark, churning river. The city lights, a distant glimmer, faded as the storm intensified, the wind whipping around them.

Ria, still perilously close to Aira, leaned out the window, the gun steady in her hand. She aimed again, her expression a mixture of rage and desperation.

Another BANG echoed across the water.

Aira's car skidded violently, a tire blowing out, sending the car spinning closer to the edge of the bridge. She fought for control, but the car lurched forward, the front end bumping against the bridge railing.

Aira, clutching her side, stumbled out of her wrecked hatchback. Her face was pale, streaked with rain and pain.

Ria emerged from her car, the gun steady in her hand, her face a storm of conflicting emotions: betrayal, rage, and a deep, wrenching sorrow. She walked towards Aira, each step measured, deliberate.

Aira, backed against the bridge railing, raised her hands in surrender. There was nowhere left to run. The wind whipped her hair across her face as she looked at Ria, a strange calmness settling over her.

V's motorcycle screeched to a stop behind them. He leaped off, dropping the bike to the asphalt. His eyes widened in horror as he took in the scene – Aira trapped, Ria's gun trained on her.

He broke into a run, adrenaline lending him speed. "Aira...move!" he shouted, his voice filled with desperation.

But it was too late. Aira just stood there, a sad smile playing on her lips. She slowly spread her arms wide, a gesture of acceptance.

As Ria stared down the barrel of the gun, fragmented images flashed through her mind: their shared childhood, Aira caring for Ria like a mother, standing by her side through thick and thin, their laughter echoing in the air.

The last image lingered – their intertwined laughter, the echo of shared joy.

A single tear rolled down Ria's cheek, mingling with the rain.

"Ria, no!" V shouted, his voice filled with a desperate plea.

As V's shout reached them, Ria closed her eyes, her finger tightening on the trigger.

Two gunshots pierced the night.

V, with a surge of superhuman strength, threw himself in front of Aira as the first shot rang out. He crumpled to the ground, clutching his chest, a crimson stain blooming on his shirt.

The second shot hit its mark.

Aira's eyes widened in surprise. She looked down at her chest, then back up at Ria and fallen V, a strange, peaceful expression washing over her face.

Slowly, almost gracefully, she began to tip backward, losing her balance as if pushed by an invisible hand.

"I...fulfilled my promise," she whispered, her words lost in the wind and rain.

Her eyes fluttered closed. With a final sigh, she disappeared over the edge of the bridge, swallowed by the darkness.

On the bridge, Ria watched, her entire body trembling, the gun slipping from her grasp and clattering to the asphalt.

V, on the ground, struggled for breath, blood seeping between his fingers. His eyes locked with Ria's.

The wail of approaching sirens grew louder, closer. Headlights appeared in the distance, cutting through the downpour. An ambulance.

Ria, without a word, turned and ran towards the approaching vehicle, her silhouette swallowed by the storm.

V watched her go, then slowly, painfully pushed himself up onto his elbows. He saw the ambulance, a beacon of hope in the distance, and then looked back at the spot where Aira disappeared.

With a groan, he collapsed back onto the asphalt, his last thought a silent plea for Aira, lost in the rain and the darkness.

The city lights blurred, the night air thick with the scent of rain and the lingering echo of the gunshots. The bridge, a silent witness to the unfolding drama, stood bathed in the eerie glow of the city lights.

The path ahead was uncertain, the future shrouded in darkness. But Ria, her heart heavy with grief, her hands stained with blood, knew she had to move forward. She had to protect V, the man who had sacrificed everything for her, the man who had loved her from the shadows. She had to find a way to bring the darkness into the light, to find a way to heal the wounds that ran deep.

CHAPTER THIRTY-THREE

"A Bridge of Light"

As V watched Ria disappear into the storm, his body wracked with pain, his mind replayed a nightmarish echo of the past. It was a scene etched in his memory, a haunting reminder of the night his world had shattered.

Rain-streaked asphalt, swirling neon reflections. V, blood staining his white shirt, stumbling through the deluge, eyes wide with pain and fear. Ria's terrified face, illuminated by approaching headlights.

The deafening screech of brakes, a blinding white light. Bodies flying, a symphony of crunching metal and shattering glass. V and Ria, sprawled on the pavement, a mangled vehicle between them. Reaching hands, fingers brushing, an impossible distance. Tears and rain, mingling on pale cheeks. Fading light, the encroaching darkness.

The montage ended abruptly, snapping back to the present. V gasped, his body racked with a fresh wave of pain. His hand, reaching for a connection that no longer existed, fell limp onto the rain-soaked asphalt.

The rain continued to fall, a relentless torrent. V lay on the asphalt, his vision graying at the edges. Each breath sent a searing pain through his chest. The ambulance siren, a distant memory, faded into the rhythm of the storm. He felt a sense of detachment, as if he were watching himself from a distance.

He blinked, trying to focus. Ria. She was sprawled a few feet away, her silhouette a broken doll against the glittering asphalt.

He tried to call out to her, but his voice was a dry croak, lost in the wind. He felt a desperate need to reach her, to know she was okay.

With agonizing slowness, fueled by adrenaline and a primal need to reach her, he tried to move. Pain exploded in his chest, pinning him to the pavement.

He saw Ria shift, her hand twitching, reaching in his direction. A surge of desperate hope flared within him.

Inch by agonizing inch, their fingers, trembling, stretched across the divide, a testament to their battered bodies and unwavering connection. They met, a fragile bridge between life and death.

The world exploded.

A low hum vibrated through the air, growing steadily louder. Both of their lockets, his resting on his chest, hers clutched in her hand, began to glow, a pulsating blue light cutting through the gloom.

Ria's eyes widened, fear and confusion battling in their depths. She saw flashes of images, heard whispers of conversations that weren't her own. V's life, his memories, his pain, began to bleed into hers.

She felt a surge of energy, a connection she couldn't explain, a feeling she couldn't deny. She saw the young boy who had saved her, the bond that had been forged between them, the love that had bloomed in the shadows. She saw his pain, his sacrifices, his unwavering devotion.

A wave of understanding washed over her, a realization of the depth of his love, a love that transcended time, space, and even the boundaries of life and death.

CHAPTER THIRTY-FOUR

"The Game of Shadows"

The air in the abandoned tunnel was thick with dust motes dancing in the single ray of sunlight that pierced the entrance. The rough concrete walls were adorned with graffiti, a canvas of faded rebellion. V stood in the center of the tunnel, his stance aggressive, his face a mask of betrayal and rage. He was a stranger to her, yet she felt an inexplicable connection to him, a sense of shared history.

Aira stood defiant, but fear flickered in her eyes as she faced V. He lunged, his movements swift and brutal. Aira dodged, her agility born of desperation.

A brutal dance unfolded. V attacked, relentless, each blow aimed to capture, to punish. Aira, smaller but quicker, evaded, her movements fueled by a desperate need to escape.

But V was relentless. He caught her, his hands clamping around her arms, spinning her around to face him. He slammed her against the damp concrete wall, his grip unyielding.

"Why, Aira?" he demanded, his voice raw with fury. "Why did you do this? You were her friend!"

Aira, her back pressed against the cold concrete, avoided his gaze, her chest heaving.

"Explain yourself!" V shouted, shaking her. "Tell me why you're hurting her!"

A slow, defiant smile spread across Aira's lips.

"I will explain," she said, her voice surprisingly calm.

Sunlight streamed through dusty windows, illuminating a lavishly furnished living room. The air was heavy with the scent of incense, a poor mask for the tension that permeated the room. Aira, small for her age, cowered on the floor, her small frame shaking with suppressed sobs. She clutched a worn teddy bear, its fur matted with tears.

Towering over her was her father, a man whose sharp features and expensive suit radiated an air of cold authority. He gripped a leather belt in his hand, the buckle gleaming ominously in the sunlight.

"Get up, Aira," he growled, his voice laced with impatience.

Aira flinched but didn't move.

"Did you not hear me?" he said, his voice rising. "On your feet! This is no way for the heir to my empire to behave!"

Aira slowly rose, her eyes downcast, her small body trembling.

"You will learn obedience, Aira," he said, pacing like a caged predator. "You will learn to respect the legacy that will one day be yours. This family business, our business...it demands strength, ruthlessness!"

"But Father," Aira said, her voice barely a whisper. "I don't want to be ruthless. I don't want your...empire. I don't want any part of your business, especially if it means doing something illegal."

She took a hesitant step back.

"What was that?" her father said, his voice sharp with displeasure.

"I want to be an archer!" Aira said, gathering her courage. "I'm good at it, Father. I've been training since I was little. Please, let me train. All those years...they'll be wasted if I have to stop now. Please, let me follow my own path."

"What did you say?!" her father roared, his eyes flashing with fury. "You dare defy me? This family's legacy...my legacy...is not a game!"

He raised the belt. Aira squeezed her eyes shut, bracing for the blow.

A hand, strong and firm, caught the belt mid-swing.

Aiden, Aira's older brother, stood between them, his face a mask of cold fury. He glared at his father, his grip on the belt tightening.

"Leave her alone," he said, his voice low and dangerous.

A tense silence gripped the room. The only sound was Aira's stifled sobs.

The Father stared at his son, a flicker of surprise crossing his features, quickly replaced by cold anger. "Let go of the belt, Aiden," he said. "This doesn't concern you."

"Everything about Aira concerns me," Aiden said, his eyes locked on his father. "Now, let her go."

The Father hesitated, then slowly lowered his hand, releasing the belt. Aiden didn't move, his eyes cold and unwavering.

Finally, with a snort of disgust, the Father turned and strode out of the room, leaving a palpable tension hanging in the air.

As soon as he was gone, Aira rushed into Aiden's arms, burying her face in his chest, her sobs now uncontainable.

Aiden held her close, his hand stroking her hair, a tenderness in his eyes that belied the steely resolve he displayed moments before. He glanced at the door, his expression hardening as a dangerous glint entered his eyes.

The room was bathed in the cool glow of moonlight filtering through the window. Aira, her face etched with worry even in sleep, tossed and turned beneath the covers.

Aira bolted upright in bed, gasping for air. A vision, fragmented and vivid, flashed before her eyes:

Aira's own face, her eyes filled with a desperate sorrow.

Two figures, a man and a woman, their faces obscured by shadow, locked in a loving embrace.

A castle inside, ancient and desolate, littered with bodies.

Aira, dressed in ornate armor, falls to her knees, a sword piercing her chest.

The fragmented images were accompanied by a voice, echoing, distorted, but filled with agonizing regret:

"I promise... If I get a second chance to help them... I will do whatever it takes to keep them happy... even if it means sacrificing myself..."

Silence. Aira gasped, her eyes wide with terror.

She stumbled out of bed, her legs unsteady, her heart pounding against her ribs like a trapped bird.

"V...Ria...Was that...another life?" she whispered to herself, her voice trembling.

The weight of the vision, its cryptic message, settled upon her like a shroud.

"Am I somehow responsible for their deaths?" she asked, a sense of dread creeping in.

She paced the room, her mind racing. The pieces didn't fit, yet they felt terrifyingly familiar.

Aira froze, listening intently. Footsteps. Muffled voices. A sense of dread washed over her.

"He's gone...he's really gone..." a woman's voice sobbed.

Aira's blood ran cold. She rushed to the door, her hand trembling as she reached for the handle.

The room was draped in white, the air thick with the scent of lilies and grief. Mourners, faces etched with sorrow, moved like shadows through the somber gathering.

Aira stood numbly near the back, her eyes fixed on a framed photograph of her father, his face frozen in a smile that seemed both unfamiliar and unsettling.

Her father was dead. Heart attack, they said. Sudden and unexpected.

"Sudden?" she whispered, a chill creeping up her spine. "Or was this the death I was supposed to prevent?"

Her gaze drifted across the room, landing on Ria. Even in mourning, Ria held herself with a quiet strength that Aira had always admired. Their eyes met across the sea of faces. Ria, her features drawn but composed, offered a sad, knowing smile.

A jolt passed through Aira. "That smile...The woman...it was her," she whispered, a sense of dread creeping in. "In the vision..."

Her doubt about V and Ria's connection deepened into a gnawing suspicion. "Were they more than friends? Is that why..."

An idea, as thrilling as it was terrifying, took root in her mind.

Aira watched from a distance as Ria gathered her things, her movements subdued, her usual energy dimmed by grief.

"Okay, Aira," she said to herself, a plan taking shape. "Think. You need to get Ria and V together. To...nudge them toward each other."

Aiden turned to Aira, a questioning look on his face. Aira pasted on a reassuring smile, hoping it masked the whirlwind of thoughts behind her eyes.

"This is my chance," she thought, a rising sense of urgency, a determination to change the course of fate.

"To see if I can change things. To fix what I might have broken."

Aiden nodded, agreeing to let her "support" Ria in the city. Aira fought back a triumphant smile.

"V, Ria," she thought, a mixture of hope and fear welling up inside her, "whatever happened between you, in that other life...this time, I'll make sure it ends differently."

Aira's gaze followed Ria as she disappeared out the door. A gamble, yes, but a gamble Aira felt compelled to take. The weight of the vision, the promise she made across lifetimes, pushed her forward.

The funeral guests thinned. Aira found Aiden near the entrance, his shoulders slumped with grief, his usual composure shaken.

She approached him quietly and embraced him, burying her face in his chest, tears welling in her eyes.

Aiden held her close, his hand stroking her hair. He whispered soothingly, his voice thick with emotion.

"It's alright, Aira. Let it out. I'm here."

He pulled back slightly, cupping her face in his hands, gently wiping away her tears. A new resolve hardened his features.

"Aira, this is your chance," he said. "You're free now. Free to follow your dreams, to make your own path. I'll take care of everything here. Don't you worry about the business."

"But...what about you?" Aira asked, her concern for her brother evident.

"Don't worry about me," Aiden said. "Focus on you. What do you want to do? What do you need?"

"I need...to focus on my archery," Aira said, her voice hesitant. "I need to train, to compete.

I...I can't do that and keep up with universitas."

"Then drop out," Aiden said, his voice firm.

"Drop out?" Aira said, her eyes widening in surprise. "But..."

Aiden smiled, a rare, genuine smile that transformed his usually stoic features. "This is your dream, Aira," he said. "Go after it with everything you have. I believe in you."

A surge of gratitude and affection washed over Aira. She threw her arms around her brother, burying her face in his shoulder.

The study, once a place of power and control, now felt cold and sterile. Moonlight spilled through the window, illuminating Aira, her face pale and drawn. She sifted through a drawer in her father's old desk, her brow furrowed in concentration.

(SOUND of footsteps approaching)

Aira froze, her head snapping up. She quickly ducked behind the heavy velvet curtains just as the door creaked open.

Aiden strode into the room, his face illuminated by the light from the hallway. Gone was the supportive brother Aira knew. In his place stood a man hardened by ambition, his eyes cold and calculating.

Manager Raju, nervous but eager to please, followed close behind.

"Everything's in place, sir," Raju said, a hint of awe in his voice. "The contracts, the endorsements...you've finally done it. You've built your empire."

Aiden moved to stand behind his father's large desk, his fingers drumming on the polished surface. He inhaled deeply, a satisfied smile spreading across his face.

"Empire, Raju," he said, his voice smooth and dangerous. "Don't diminish it. This is more than just a business. This...this is a dynasty."

He paused, his smile turning predatory. "And it took sacrifice. Calculated risks."

"About that, sir," Raju said nervously. "I can't help but feel...uneasy. We've hurt a lot of people to get here. Good people. Athletes who deserved their chance."

"There's no room for sentiment in this business, Raju," Aiden said, his eyes hardening.

"Only winners and losers. And I don't intend to be a loser."

"You certainly were ruthless in dealing with your father," Raju said, a touch of admiration in his voice. "And manipulating your own sister...brilliant, sir, truly brilliant."

Aira, hidden behind the curtain, gasps softly. Her heart pounds in her chest, a drumbeat of betrayal.

"But how...?" Raju asked, struggling to comprehend the ruthlessness. "How could you? He was your own father."

"He left me no choice," Aiden said, a chilling chuckle escaping his lips.

The room was thick with cigar smoke. Aira's father sat behind the desk, his face half-shadowed, a glass of amber liquid in his hand. Aiden, his face flushed with anger, paced before him.

"You still don't understand," the Father said, his voice laced with disdain. "You're weak, Aiden. Sentimental. You actually believe in things like...fairness, integrity."

"And you don't?" Aiden asked, his voice cracking with anger.

"Those are liabilities in this business!" the Father said, a cruel laugh escaping his lips.

"Aira...she understands. She has the ruthlessness I need in an heir. You...you're nothing but a disappointment."

The Father turned his back on Aiden, reaching for a cigar from a humidor on his desk. The dismissal stung more than any blow.

Aiden's hand trembled as he grabbed a heavy marble ashtray from a side table. He took a step closer to his father, his face a mask of rage and hurt.

(The scene unfold back to the present before Aiden strikes, leaving the act of violence to the audience's imagination.)

Aiden took a drag from his own cigarette, his face illuminated by the orange glow. The resemblance to his father in that moment was chilling.

"He underestimated me," Aiden said, exhaling a plume of smoke. "Just like everyone else."

"But your sister...she's on the verge of national recognition," Raju said nervously. "What if she decides she wants back in?"

"Aira is nothing but a pawn in my game, Raju," Aiden said, his eyes hardening. "A useful

distraction. She'll never be a threat to me."

"But what about her friend...Ria?" Raju asked, frowning. "What if she wins the competition?"

Aiden's face contorted into a mask of pure fury. He slammed his fist on the desk, making Raju jump.

"Ria is a problem I intend to solve," he said, his voice dangerously low.

He leaned forward, his voice barely a whisper. "Tomorrow. We make sure Ria never picks up a bow and arrow again."

Aiden and Raju exited the study, leaving Aira hidden behind the curtain, her blood running cold.

Aira emerged from behind the curtain, tears streaming down her face. Her brother's words,"Tomorrow. We make sure Ria never picks up a bow and arrow again," echoed in her ears, each syllable a hammer blow to her heart.

"Tomorrow..." she whispered to herself. "He's going to hurt her. I have to stop him. But how?"

Her gaze fell on her father's desk, the surface scattered with contracts and files – the remnants of the empire built on lies and ruthlessness.

"Aiden isn't the only one who can play this game," she whispered, a spark of determination igniting in her eyes.

Aira swiftly sifted through her father's old files, her fingers tracing the names of clients, investors, even rivals. She found what she's looking for: a discreet business card tucked into a folder labeled "Security."

"My father always believed in having...contingencies," she said to herself. "People who could handle problems discreetly."

Aira, her face illuminated by the glow of her phone, made a call, her voice low and urgent.

"Aiden might have inherited his business sense," she said, her voice steely with determination. "But these...connections...they still answer to the name Avani."

Aira carefully placed a gift at V's home outside. Inside, a single ticket to the archery competition—Ria's competition. She knew V wouldn't ignore this. She had to trust her instincts, her intuition, that this was the best way to protect Ria.

The sound of a DOORBELL ringing)

(MONTAGE FLASHBACK ENDS)

Aira sat in the back seat of a nondescript car, her face a mask of anxiety and regret. She watched through the tinted windows as a group of men surrounded Ria's car, their movements swift and brutal.

"I tried to stop it," she whispered, her voice laced with guilt. "I hired those men to scare her, to delay her, not to..."

A gut-wrenching CRACK echoed through the car as one of the men smashed the driver's side window of Ria's car. Aira flinched, her hand flying to her mouth to stifle a gasp.

"I didn't think he'd go that far," she said, her voice cracking. "That he'd break her fingers."

The scene shifted abruptly. Years had passed. Aira was watching V and Ria from a distance – at a park, in a cafe, at Ria's birthday surprise, always a silent observer.

"I watched over you both, from the shadows," Aira said, a bittersweet ache in her voice. "I needed to make sure you were safe, happy...especially Ria. And V...I recognized you, even with the changes you'd made. You were still the Rohan I once knew, but...different. Stronger. Kinder. And seeing you protect her, care for her...it gave me a sliver of hope in all the darkness."

The flashback within a flashback ended.

The air felt heavy with anticipation. Aira, having witnessed the depth of V's sacrifice, the intensity of his love for Ria, felt a renewed sense of hope. She had to act, to intervene, to try to change the course of their destiny. She knew that the truth about V's identity, the connection they shared, could bring them together. And perhaps, by bringing them together, she could undo the damage she had done, the mistakes she had made. She had to try. She had to make things right.

CHAPTER THIRTY-FIVE

"The Weight of Truth"

The air in the abandoned tunnel was thick with the scent of decay and the metallic tang of blood. V, his body bruised and aching, stared at Aira. The woman he'd known, the one who'd shown him kindness, had just confessed to a life of unimaginable darkness.

"What have you done?" he whispered, his voice hoarse with disbelief.

Aira, her face streaked with tears, looked at him with a mixture of pain and defiance. "I did what I had to do," she said, her voice wavering. "To protect her. To make amends for my mistakes."

The weight of her confession pressed down on V like a physical force. Aiden, the man he'd considered a friend, had been a monster, a manipulator, and Aira, the woman he'd thought was innocent, was his accomplice. He felt a wave of nausea rise in his throat, the truth churning like a storm in his stomach.

"What about my father?" V asked, his voice choked with anger. "Did Aiden kill him?"

Aira closed her eyes, a single tear tracing a path down her cheek. "No. He didn't kill your father. I did."

The words hung in the air, heavy with the weight of a lifetime's guilt. V stared at her, unable to comprehend the darkness that had consumed her.

"You... you killed my father?"

"That night, the accident, it wasn't an accident. I hired those men to get to Aiden. But your father... he got caught in the crossfire."

A silence descended, heavy and oppressive. The dripping water echoed in the stillness, each drop a solemn beat in the symphony of their grief.

"And Ria's parents," Aira continued, her voice hollow, her words a litany of past sins. "Their accident... that was my fault too. I was a child, but I made a stupid, careless mistake. I damaged an important file in my father's office. The head manager forced Ria's father to come back to the office that night to fix it. He said it was urgent, there was going to be a raid. And then... the accident happened. I didn't know how to fix it. I was so scared. So, I kept quiet."

Aira's confessions unfolded like a tapestry woven from the threads of darkness and regret.

Each revelation was a blow to V's heart, a shattering of the fragile hope he'd clung to. He sank to the floor, his eyes fixed on Aira, his heart aching with a profound sense of betrayal and loss.

"I... I kidnapped you, V," Aira said, her voice barely a whisper. "I needed you to know the truth. To understand."

The weight of Aira's confession pressed down on V, suffocating him with a mixture of horror and disbelief. He couldn't grasp the depths of her pain, the years of hidden darkness she carried within her. It was too much.

Suddenly, the headlights of a car sliced through the darkness at the tunnel's entrance. The engine cut out, plunging them back into a deeper silence, broken only by the dripping water. Aiden stepped out of the shadows, his smile chillingly familiar, a mix of charm and menace.

"Well, well," he said, his voice dripping with venomous amusement. "Look who decided to show their face. Right on schedule."

His eyes met Aira's, a glint of triumph shimmering in their depths. "And you, dear sister.

Always a talent for dramatic entrances. Did you enjoy the show?"

Aira stepped forward, shielding V with her body. "Leave him alone, Aiden. This ends now."

Aiden chuckled, his laughter echoing in the confines of the tunnel. "End? Darling, we're just getting started. I have a special treat planned for you. A little... punishment... for your betrayal. But first..."

He gestured towards V, his eyes cold and menacing. "Take care of him. Make it hurt."

The mercenaries, their faces grim and hardened, advanced on V. Aira's heart pounded in her chest, fear tightening her throat.

"V, be careful!" she pleaded, her voice laced with desperation.

V met her gaze, a strange calmness settling over him. He offered her a reassuring smile, his eyes steady. "Don't worry about me," he whispered.

He turned to face the mercenaries, his body loose and relaxed, his eyes assessing their every move. The fight that ensued was brutal, a dance of desperation and raw power. The tunnel became a cage, its walls closing in on them, amplifying the echoes of their struggle.

Aiden watched, a cold smile curving his lips. "You fight like an amateur," he sneered, his voice dripping with contempt. "All that rage, so... uncontrolled."

He moved with surprising speed and agility, landing blow after blow on V, his strength relentless. V fought back with desperate fury, but Aiden was stronger, more ruthless.

Finally, with a swift kick to V's stomach, Aiden sent him crashing to the ground. Aira watched in horror as Aiden grabbed a discarded metal pipe from the tunnel floor, a glint of cold steel in the flickering light.

He raised the pipe, his face contorted with a chilling mix of rage and triumph. "Any last words, brother?" he asked, his voice a menacing whisper.

Aira knew this was it. Her brother, consumed by darkness, was about to kill V. She acted instinctively, driven by a desperate need to protect the man she'd wronged, the man who'd become entangled in her web of guilt and atonement.

With a strangled cry, she grabbed a discarded knife from the ground, a forgotten relic of Aiden's cruelty. She lunged, her small frame propelled by a surge of adrenaline and fear.

The knife plunged into Aiden's back. He froze, a gasp escaping his lips. He slowly turned, his eyes wide with shock and disbelief, staring at the woman who dared to defy him, to betray him.

"Aira... you...," he choked, his voice a rasping whisper.

He crumpled to the ground, the metal pipe clattering beside him. Aira stood over him, her body shaking, the bloody knife trembling in her hand. The enormity of what she'd done crashed over her, a wave of guilt and despair.

V, struggling to his feet, looked on in stunned silence. "Aira... what have you done?" he asked, his voice hoarse.

Aira dropped the knife, the metallic clang echoing through the tunnel. Tears streamed down her face, but her voice was steady. "It started with me... with my mistakes. Let me bring it to an end."

She took a deep breath, composing herself. Time was running out. "Go, V," she said, her voice laced with urgency. "Today is the match. The final selection for the national team. You have to be there. For Ria."

V hesitated, torn between his concern for Aira and the urgency in her voice. He knew he couldn't force her. Not now. He nodded, his heart heavy with a premonition he couldn't quite place. "I'll be back," he promised.

He turned and ran towards the light at the end of the tunnel, leaving Aira standing alone in the darkness, the weight of her choices heavy on her shoulders.

The weight of her actions pressed down on Aira, a suffocating blanket of guilt and responsibility. As V disappeared into the tunnel, a chilling resolve settled over her. It was time to make amends, to right the wrongs she'd committed, even if it meant sacrificing everything she had left.

She moved with a practiced efficiency, a stark contrast to the trembling woman she had been moments before. She retrieved a worn leather briefcase from her father's old office, a briefcase filled with documents, files, and a hidden compartment containing a thick wad of cash. It was her father's "dirty money," a testament to his life of ruthless ambition and shadowy dealings. Now, it would be used to atone for his sins and her own.

Aira left the tunnel and found herself back on the familiar, deserted streets of the city. She navigated the labyrinthine alleys and backstreets she had known since childhood, her movements purposeful and confident.

She reached the imposing steel and glass structure of her father's office building, a monument to his ambition and wealth. The building was silent and deserted, the lights dimmed, the air thick with a stale, artificial smell. Aira knew every corner, every hidden passage, every secret room. She slipped through the back entrance, her movements silent and precise.

Inside, the office was a tomb of ambition, filled with expensive furniture, art, and the faint scent of power. Aira walked past the portraits of her father, their cold eyes following her every move. She reached the back room, a hidden chamber concealed behind a bookcase. This was her father's personal sanctum, a room filled with private files, hidden accounts, and a reinforced safe that housed his most valuable assets.

The cold steel of the safe yielded to the touch of her father's keys, keys she had taken from his desk long ago, anticipating this day. She carefully removed the contents of the safe, transferring them to her briefcase. As she closed the safe, a feeling of closure washed over her. It was done. The past, her father's legacy, would be buried with him.

Back in her apartment, Aira moved through the shadows, the dim light from the city illuminating her face. She placed her briefcase on the coffee table and picked up the phone. Her first call was to a financial advisor, a man who had handled her father's investments for years. Her voice was firm, her words precise.

"I need you to liquidate everything," she instructed, her voice cold and emotionless. "The accounts, the properties, the investments... everything."

The advisor, surprised by her abrupt tone, offered a few questions, but Aira silenced him.

"I need this done immediately," she said, her voice cold and uncompromising.

Her next call was to the head of her father's security detail, a man who knew the intricate web of connections her father had built over the years.

"I need you to arrange for a discreet dispersal of the funds," she instructed, her voice unwavering. "Distribute the funds to our employees, severance packages, pensions... whatever they are owed. The rest... donate it. To charities. Orphanages. Whatever you think is right."

The final call was to the manager who handled her father's less savory dealings, the man who had been privy to her father's darkest secrets. He was a man of few words, efficient and ruthless, the perfect person for the job she had in mind.

"There's one more thing," she said, her voice a blend of determination and resignation. "I need you to draw up some documents. A transfer of ownership. The office building... I want to turn it into a... a home. For disabled children. People like Ria."

The manager, a man who had witnessed countless power plays, was taken aback by her request.

"But madam," he said, his voice laced with confusion, "we need your brother's signature for
that."

Aira's face softened, a bittersweet smile gracing her lips. "Don't worry," she said, her voice low and soothing. "I took care of that a long time ago."

The manager, a man who had seen his fair share of deceit and treachery, didn't press further.

He understood. He would handle the details, ensure the transaction was completed as instructed.

With the final call made, Aira felt a sense of liberation, a release from the burden she had carried for so long. She had taken the first steps towards atoning for her mistakes. She knew it wasn't enough, but it was a start.

Now, all she could do was wait. Wait for V to return, to fulfill his promise. Wait to see if the seeds she had sown would bear fruit. Wait to see if the darkness that had consumed her life could finally be replaced with the hope of a future, a future that, for the first time in her life, she dared to believe in.

CHAPTER THIRTY-SIX

"The Masks of Fate"

The rain had stopped, leaving behind an almost unnatural silence. The street, once a vibrant artery of the city, was now a desolate tableau of twisted metal and shattered glass. V and Ria lay amidst the wreckage of the truck, their bodies battered, their breathing shallow. A faint blue glow emanated from the locket, illuminating their intertwined fingers, a silent testament to the bond that held them together even in death.

The memories, Aira's memories, flooded through Ria's consciousness. The tidal wave of guilt, sacrifice, and love left her breathless, a crushing weight upon her soul. Tears streamed down her face, mingling with the rain that had begun to fall again, a gentle, cleansing rain.

She opened her eyes, meeting V's gaze. His eyes, filled with concern, mirrored her own pain, a shared understanding of their impending fate. Across the chasm of their imminent deaths, they found forgiveness, gratitude, and a love that transcended lifetimes.

Their grip tightened, a silent vow. They held on to each other, clinging to the warmth of their connection, their breaths becoming shallower, their hearts beating slower.

And then, as if a force beyond their control was pulling their souls from their broken bodies, their eyes lost focus. Their hands went limp, their bodies still, their breathing fading into silence.

Two figures, ethereal and translucent, shimmered into existence beside them. A male spirit and a female spirit, their forms radiating a sorrow that seemed both ancient and unending. They watched the lifeless forms of V and Ria, their faces etched with grief, their eyes reflecting a depth of pain that spoke to centuries of suffering.

The male spirit knelt beside Ria, his hand hovering over hers, his touch soft and reverent.

The female spirit knelt beside V, mirroring the gesture, her hand hovering over his, a silent promise of comfort.

As the light faded, the male and female spirits found themselves in a familiar yet chilling setting: the scene of the car crash. They were solid, flesh and blood once more, but trapped in the moment of their deaths.

The female spirit gasped, her hands flying to her face, her eyes wide with shock and confusion. The male spirit cried out, a raw, primal sound of anguish, a sound that echoed the agony of their loss.

They were V and Ria, their positions mirroring their lifeless forms on the bridge above, their bodies trapped in the moment of their demise. Yet, their faces were hidden behind ornate, full-face masks, their features obscured by the intricate carvings of the masks. The masks were beautiful, crafted with exquisite detail, but they radiated an oppressive sorrow, echoing the tragedy of their deaths.

Slowly, almost reluctantly, they turned towards each other, their eyes meeting, a silent exchange of shock and confusion.

The masks, as if imbued with a life of their own, began to crack, a spiderweb of fractures appearing across their surface. The cracks glowed with a faint blue light, like veins of pure energy, emanating from within.

With a sudden, shattering force, the masks exploded outward, a shower of glittering fragments cascading around them. The faces revealed beneath were not exact replicas, but they were undeniably, heartbreakingly familiar.

The man's face, now free of the mask, bore a striking resemblance to V. The same strong jawline, the same intense eyes, but a weariness in his gaze, a depth of sorrow that spoke to centuries of suffering.

The woman's face mirrored Ria's delicate features. The same high cheekbones, the same kind eyes, but her expression was etched with a haunting sadness, a reflection of lifetimes lost to a cruel twist of fate.

They stared at each other, their faces illuminated by the flickering headlights of the wrecked car, their eyes wide with shock and dawning recognition. Their hearts, once still and silent, began to beat again, a rhythmic echo of their shared past, their shared fate.

The world faded to black, leaving them suspended in that moment of recognition, the weight of their past, their present, and their future pressing down on them, a burden they would carry for eternity.

CHAPTER THIRTY-SEVEN

"The Crown of Ashes"

The ancient map of the world unfurled itself, a tapestry of parchment and ink, painted with the echoes of forgotten battles and whispered legends. Three kingdoms, each represented by a unique emblem, dominated its expanse.

Lunaria, the kingdom of the moon, bore a crescent moon, its silver now tarnished, the edges cracked and faded, a symbol of a kingdom on the brink of ruin. Solara, the kingdom of the sun, was represented by a gleaming golden serpent, coiled and poised to strike, its scales shimmering with an ambition that threatened to consume all. And Eldoria, the kingdom of the stars, was marked by a stylized sun, its fiery rays reaching out, a beacon of hidden strength.

lingered on Lunaria's emblem, the cracks in the crescent moon seeming to spread, a tangible representation of the kingdom's vulnerability. Then, the focus shifted, sweeping across the map towards a specific point within Lunaria's borders, a point that held the key to the kingdom's future.

Dust swirled in the air, a pale brown cloud billowing above the battered training grounds of Lunaria. Miyu, the princess, her features sharp and determined, her eyes blazing with a fire that mirrored the flames licking at the tips of the arrows she fired, moved with the practiced grace of a warrior. Years of relentless training had honed her skills, transformed her into a weapon, a force to be reckoned with.

Each arrow, imbued with fire, found its mark in the heart of a straw-stuffed dummy, a testament to her unwavering precision. The dummies, riddled with past hits, bore the scars of her training, a silent chronicle of her dedication.

Finally, she lowered her bow, her chest heaving, her muscles aching with the exertion. Sweat glistened on her brow, a testament to her unwavering commitment.

A timid maid, her eyes downcast, approached Miyu. "Princess Miyu? The ministers request your presence. They await you in the council chambers."

Miyu nodded curtly, her face hardened, her expression a mask of controlled anger. She shed her training leathers, revealing a simple but elegant gown underneath, a stark contrast to the warrior she had become.

She strode into the ruined palace, her bearing regal despite the destruction surrounding her.

The palace, once a magnificent monument to Lunaria's glory, was now a testament to Solara's brutal conquest. The walls were scarred, the ceilings cracked, the windows shattered, remnants of a once powerful kingdom crumbling into dust.

The council chambers, once a place of diplomacy and power, were now dim and scarred, a reflection of the kingdom's weakened state. Two ministers, their faces etched with worry, sat at a table piled high with scrolls, their shoulders slumped with the weight of their responsibility.

Miyu entered, her chin held high, her gaze unwavering. She didn't wait for an invitation but fixed her eyes on the elder minister, her expression a challenge.

"You wanted to see me?" she asked, her voice firm, her tone laced with a hint of impatience.

"I trust this concerns the matter of the throne."

The elder minister, his face creased with age and concern, cleared his throat. "Indeed, Princess. We have... concerns. This matter is not so simple."

Miyu's eyes flashed with anger. "Concerns? My father named me heir. What more is there to discuss?"

The younger minister, unable to meet her gaze, spoke up. "Lunaria lies in ruins, Princess.

King Daichi of Solara... he left us with nothing. Your father... he..."

Miyu's hand clenched into a fist, her nails digging into her palm, a testament to the anger that burned within her. "He was murdered by young Daichi ," she said, her voice sharp and clipped. "I am well aware of what transpired here. Don't speak of it as if it were ancient history."

"The people are afraid, Miyu," the elder minister said, his voice laced with a concern that bordered on desperation. "They need more than a grieving daughter. They need a leader who can unite them, who can avenge them."

Miyu's chest swelled with indignation. "And I will lead them!" she declared, her voice ringing with a fierce determination. "I have trained for this my entire life!"

"But they will not follow, not yet," the younger minister said, his voice barely a whisper. "Not while Daichi lives. Not while the fear of Solara hangs over us."

Miyu's jaw tightened, her eyes narrowed, a flicker of defiance in their depths. "What would you have me do? Beg for their approval?"

The elder minister leaned forward, his gaze unwavering. "Earn it," he said, his voice a low rumble. "Show them you are the leader your father believed you to be. Go to Solara. End Daichi 's reign.

Free us from this terror. Then, and only then, will you be their Queen."

A flicker of something dangerous sparked in Miyu's eyes, a hint of the warrior she had become, a warrior who was ready to take on the world.

"You ask me to kill a king?" she asked, her voice a mixture of challenge and intrigue. "To walk into the lion's den?"

"We ask you to reclaim what is rightfully yours," the elder minister said, his voice steady and unwavering. "To avenge your father, and to secure your throne."

Miyu stood for a moment, weighing their words, her mind racing, her heart pounding. The weight of their request, the burden of responsibility, pressed down on her, a heavy cloak of destiny.

Then, with a resolute nod, she spoke, her voice echoing in the ruined hall, a declaration of war, a promise of vengeance.

"So be it," she said, her voice echoing with a newfound confidence. "Daichi stole my birthright and took my father from me. I will have my due."

CHAPTER THIRTY-EIGHT

"The Serpent's Shadow"

The map of the land, an ancient tapestry of parchment and ink, unfurled itself before the viewer. lingered on the ruined kingdom of Lunaria, its crescent moon, once a symbol of hope, now a testament to despair. With a dramatic sweep, moved across the map, settling on the gleaming kingdom of Eldoria, its stylized sun a beacon of hope in a world consumed by darkness.

Eldoria, a bustling city filled with the vibrant energy of a thriving kingdom, was a world away from the desolation of Lunaria. The air thrummed with the sounds of commerce, the aroma of spices and fresh bread filling the nostrils, the voices of vendors and patrons creating a harmonious symphony of life.

Evelyn, her face weathered by years of hardship, navigated the bustling marketplace, her brow furrowed with worry. She approached a group of men lounging by a fruit stall, their faces relaxed, their bodies radiating the carefree energy of a people who had found peace.

"Have any of you seen Kai?" she asked, her voice a mixture of concern and desperation.

The men glanced at her, their eyes disinterested, their bodies unmoving. "Can't say we have," one of them said, his voice indifferent.

"Probably down by the waterfall again," another chimed in, a hint of amusement in his tone.

"Always did like the water, that boy."

Evelyn sighed, her shoulders slumping with the weight of her anxiety. She muttered a thank you before hurrying towards the river, a sense of urgency driving her forward.

She found Kai by the waterfall, a picturesque cascade of water that seemed to embody the beauty and serenity he craved. He sat beneath the falls, the water cascading over him, washing away his worries, his face lit by a carefree grin.

"Kai!" she called out, her voice tinged with a sharpness that startled him. "Where are you? Come on, we need to go home."

Kai peeked out from behind the cascading water, his smile unwavering. "Why the rush, mother? Let me enjoy the day! I'll be back soon."

"Kai! This is important," Evelyn said, her voice firm, her tone leaving no room for argument. "Come here now!"

Kai, startled by her unusual tone, scrambled out of the water, his carefree demeanor replaced by a flicker of concern. "Alright, alright! I'm coming," he said, hurrying towards her, dripping water and worry.

Inside their modest dwelling, Evelyn dried Kai's hair with a cloth, her touch gentle despite
the anxiety that gnawed at her heart.

"What's going on, Mother?" Kai asked, his voice laced with concern. "What's so urgent?"

Evelyn held out a sealed letter, its wax seal unbroken, its contents a mystery. Kai took it, confusion clouding his features. "What is this?" he asked, his voice a mixture of curiosity and apprehension.

"Read it," Evelyn said, her eyes filled with a lifetime of unspoken truths. "But be warned, Kai... what you read will change everything."

Kai hesitated, his hand trembling slightly, his mind racing with questions. He broke the seal, revealing the parchment within. He scanned the letter, his brow furrowing, his expression a mixture of confusion and growing apprehension.

"Your presence is requested at the Eldoria Palace," he read aloud, his voice echoing in the stillness of their home. "The King wishes to discuss a matter of great importance. Come alone."

"Why would the King ask for me?" he asked, his voice laced with confusion.

Evelyn looked at him, her eyes filled with a lifetime of unspoken truths, her gaze holding a mixture of sadness and hope. "The King... he is your grandfather, Kai," she said, her voice soft but firm.

Kai stared at her, his mind reeling, his heart pounding with a mixture of disbelief and a flicker of something akin to hope. "What? What are you saying?"

"Your father... he was the King's son," Evelyn said, her voice low, a whisper that resonated with the weight of a lifetime of secrets. "We fell in love, but your grandfather forbade us from marrying. I was a commoner, unworthy in his eyes. He disowned your father and banished us from the castle."

"My father... never said a word," Kai said, his voice a whisper of shock and disbelief.

"He carried that pain with him always," Evelyn said, her voice laced with a bittersweet sadness. "But you, Kai... you are his legacy. And I believe your grandfather knows this. That is why he has summoned you."

Kai's mind raced, the weight of his mother's revelation pressing down on him, a burden he had never anticipated. He looked from the letter to his mother, his heart pounding with a mix of anger, confusion, and a flicker of something akin to hope.

The imposing structure of the Eldoria Palace loomed before him, a testament to the King's power and authority. Kai stood before the King, his grandfather, who sat upon his throne, his features bearing the marks of age and time, but his eyes still radiating the authority of a warrior.

"Welcome, Kai," the King said, his voice a deep rumble that echoed through the chamber.

"Enough with the pleasantries, Grandfather," Kai said, his voice tight with barely suppressed fury. "Let's get straight to the point."

The King's expression didn't waver, his gaze steady and unwavering. He gestured for Kai to come closer, his hand a silent invitation to share his burden.

"So you know the truth," the King said, his voice a blend of resignation and a flicker of hope. "Good. Then you also know the humiliation our kingdom has endured. Yes, we have our freedom, but at what cost? We are but puppets, paying tribute to Solara, to that tyrant Daichi ."

He slammed his fist on the armrest, his voice laced with bitter anger, his body wracked with the pain of a kingdom in chains. "Your father... he died fighting for our freedom. We lost that battle, Kai.

And we were forced to make a deal: resources, gold, anything they demanded... in exchange for a semblance of peace."

"And what does any of this have to do with me?" Kai asked, his voice sharp, his patience wearing thin.

"I am an old man, Kai," the King said, his voice weary, his eyes reflecting a lifetime of hardship. "My days are numbered. But you... you carry the blood of kings in your veins. You have a chance to claim your birthright."

"What are you suggesting?" Kai asked, his voice laced with suspicion, his heart pounding with a mixture of fear and a flicker of hope.

"Bring me Daichi ," the King said, his voice a low rumble that echoed through the chamber.

"Alive. Deliver him to me, and this throne, this kingdom, will be yours."

Kai scoffed, his head shaking in disbelief. "And what if I refuse?" he asked, his voice laced with a defiance he hadn't realized he possessed.

The King leaned forward.rd, his gaze unwavering, his voice a whisper that carried the weight of centuries of tradition. "Don't be foolish, Kai," he said, his voice a blend of persuasion and threat. "You love your mother. Don't you want to see her living here, in the palace that is rightfully hers? This is your chance to right the wrongs of the past, to avenge your father... to be the King you were born to be."

Silence hung heavy in the air, the weight of the King's words pressing down on Kai, the weight of his legacy demanding his attention. He struggled with his emotions, his heart a maelstrom of conflicting emotions: anger, fear, a flicker of hope, a yearning for a father he never knew, a desire for a life he never imagined.

Finally, he looked up, a steely glint in his eyes, a determination hardening his features. "I will bring you Daichi ," he said, his voice firm, his tone a declaration of his intentions. "And then, this throne will be mine."

Kai turned and strode out of the throne room, his head held high, his steps purposeful, his heart a maelstrom of conflicting emotions. He was a pawn in a game he didn't understand, a player in a story he hadn't chosen, but he was ready to play his part.

He found his mother at their home, their modest dwelling a stark contrast to the grandeur of the palace. He stood before her, his face drawn, his expression a mixture of determination and uncertainty.

Evelyn studied him, her eyes filled with a lifetime of unspoken truths, a mother's intuition whispering to her about the path her son had chosen.

"Go, Kai," she said, her voice a blend of concern and acceptance. "But remember... it is not the destination that matters, but the journey. Find your truth on the path ahead."

Kai didn't understand her words, but he nodded, accepting her blessing, her unspoken wisdom. He turned and walked away, his figure disappearing into the bustling streets of Eldoria, a young man embarking on a journey that would forever change his destiny.

The open gates of Eldoria, a gateway to a world of danger and intrigue, awaited him. Kai, astride a powerful horse, rode towards them, leaving the only home he'd ever known behind. He glanced back one last time, his expression a mixture of determination and uncertainty, before urging his horse forward, into the unknown, towards a destiny he could barely comprehend.

CHAPTER THIRTY-NINE

"THE SERPENT'S DANCE"

Solara, a kingdom bathed in the golden light of ambition, throbbed with life. The streets, a vibrant tapestry of commerce and celebration, echoed with the laughter of children, the cries of vendors, and the rhythmic beat of a thousand heartbeats.

Kai, weary from his journey, rode his horse through the throngs of people, his senses alert, his gaze searching for any sign of danger. Across the street, Miyu, her face a mask of controlled fury, moved with a cautious grace, her eyes scanning the crowd, her heart ablaze with a desire for vengeance.

Their paths crossed, their eyes meeting for a fleeting moment, their gaze a silent exchange of unspoken intentions. But they did not acknowledge each other, their paths diverging, their destinies intertwined yet seemingly divergent.

Kai's eyes, honed by years of wilderness survival, spotted a commotion near the city square.

Guards, their faces stern and authoritative, were recruiting soldiers for the King's army, their voices booming through the square, their words laced with promises of glory and riches.

"This is it," Kai thought, his mind racing, his heart pounding with a newfound determination. "My chance to get inside the palace. If I can become his soldier, I can get close to Daichi .

Then, I'll take him."

He spurred his horse forward, eager to join the throng of hopeful recruits, but a stern guard, his face a mask of authority, barred his way. "Hold it right there!" he boomed, his voice echoing through the square.

"You're too late. Registration is closed."

Kai, his frustration mounting, reined in his horse, his eyes scanning the faces of the other men who were ushered through the palace gates, his mind searching for an alternative.

Across the square, Miyu noticed a similar recruitment taking place, but this time for female dancers and servants. She mingled with the group of hopeful candidates, her face a mask of serenity, her eyes cold and calculating.

"A dancer... perfect," she thought, her mind already mapping out her strategy. "I'll be his shadow, close enough to strike. This palace will be Daichi 's tomb."

With a confident smile, she joined the line of women, her eyes scanning the faces of the other hopeful candidates, her gaze searching for any sign of weakness, any opportunity to exploit.

Suddenly, a hush fell over the crowd. Trumpets blared, a majestic fanfare announcing a royal arrival.

"Make way for King Daichi !" a soldier shouted, his voice echoing through the square, his words carrying a mixture of awe and fear. "And his most esteemed sister, Princess Akira !"

Kai watched from the sidelines, his jaw clenched tight, his eyes narrowed as a magnificent chariot, drawn by six white horses, pulled into the square. Daichi , Aiden, his face a mask of arrogance and power, stood tall, his hand resting on the hilt of his sword, his eyes radiating a cold authority that chilled Kai's soul.

Behind him, on an ornately decorated elephant, sat Akira , Aira, her features regal, her eyes scanning the crowd, a queen in waiting, her heart harboring secrets only she knew.

"People of Solara!" Daichi boomed, his voice reverberating through the square, his words laced with a chilling confidence. "I, your King, stand before you victorious! All kingdoms tremble before me! This is the legacy that made me even better than my father, and I will see it endure!"

Kai listened, his jaw clenched tight, his heart heavy with the weight of the oppression he witnessed. He saw the fear in the eyes of the crowd, the same fear that had crippled his own people, the same fear that drove him to seek vengeance.

"And today, I bring you joyful news!" Daichi continued, his voice a blend of authority and a touch of theatricality. "My beloved sister, Akira , is to be wed! Let the festivities begin!"

A collective gasp rose from the crowd, a mixture of awe and apprehension. Miyu, her blood running cold, her anger simmering beneath the surface, seethed with a desire to end Daichi 's reign of terror.

Her eyes, sharp and focused, noticed a heavy wooden post, held upright by ropes, positioned precariously close to where Daichi addressed the crowd.

"He revels in his tyranny, while my people suffer," she thought, her mind racing, her heart pounding with a fierce determination. "This ends now."

With lightning speed, she pulled a small, sharp blade from her robes, a weapon she had hidden for this moment, her movements swift and precise. She began sawing away at the rope securing the post, her movements quick and silent, her determination unwavering.

Kai, too, was watching the post, his eyes drawn to its instability, his senses alert. He sensed danger, but from whom, he couldn't tell. His mind raced, trying to decipher the source of the threat, his instincts warning him of imminent peril.

As the rope snapped, the massive beam began to topple towards the unsuspecting Daichi , its weight a silent promise of destruction.

"No!" Kai shouted, his voice a gasp of horror, his heart leaping into his throat.

Without hesitation, he leaped from the crowd, his body propelled by an adrenaline-fueled instinct, his mind filled with a primal desire to protect the man who held his destiny in his hands. He landed on Daichi's chariot, his movements fluid and graceful, a

seasoned warrior even though he had never seen a battle. He pulled Daichi away from the falling post just as it crashed to the ground with a deafening boom, a
testament to the power of fate and the fragility of life.

Miyu watched in astonishment, her mind struggling to grasp the speed of his movements, the power of his intervention. She couldn't see who had intervened, her vision obscured by the chaos of the falling post.

Akira , however, had a clear view of the stranger who had saved her brother. Their eyes met for a fleeting moment, a silent exchange of gratitude and intrigue, their souls touching across the distance of their conflicting loyalties.

Daichi , momentarily stunned, recovered quickly, his instincts honed by a lifetime of maneuvering through danger. He pushed the guards who rushed to attack Kai aside, his voice a commanding roar.

"Hold!" he shouted, his voice echoing through the square, his command silencing the chaos.

"Do not harm him! You... you saved my life. Name your reward! Anything!"

Kai, catching his breath, rose from his crouched position, his mind racing, a plan forming in his mind. "This is my chance," he thought, his heart pounding with a mixture of fear and a flicker of hope.

"Your Majesty," he said, his voice calm and confident, his gaze unwavering. "I seek only to serve. Let me be your bodyguard, a soldier in your army."

Daichi raised an eyebrow, his face a mask of intrigue, his mind analyzing the stranger before him. "A soldier? You ask for little... yet you risk much," he said, his voice a blend of amusement and respect. "Very well. What is your name, brave stranger?"

"I am Kai," Kai said, his voice a low rumble, his eyes meeting Daichi 's gaze, a silent challenge hidden beneath the surface.

Daichi nodded, a glint of respect flickering in his eyes, a hint of admiration for the man who had so readily risked his life for him. "Then rise, Kai, as my protector."

Kai mounted Daichi 's chariot, his senses on high alert, his heart pounding with a mixture of trepidation and excitement. He scanned the faces in the crowd, his gaze sharp and wary, searching for any lingering threat to the king.

Then, as if pulled by an invisible thread, his eyes landed on Miyu. The world around him seemed to fade away. The clamor of the crowd, the scent of spices in the air, the weight of the sword at his side – all of it disappeared. All that remained was the breathtaking vision of the woman before him.

Miyu, still caught in the aftermath of her failed attempt, felt a gaze upon her, heavy and intense. She looked up, her heart pounding, and met Kai's eyes across the throng of people. Their gazes locked, their souls colliding in that shared moment of recognition.

Time seemed to stop. The air crackled with an unexpected energy, an invisible force pulling them together, their destinies intertwined in a way neither could have anticipated. He was struck by the fire in her eyes, the intensity of her gaze, the unspoken anger simmering beneath the surface.

The chariot, with Kai now beside Daichi and Akira 's elephant following close behind, began to move, heading towards the palace. Miyu, still shaken by the intensity of their encounter, her heart pounding with a mix of confusion and a flicker of hope, joined the procession of servants and dancers, her movements fluid and graceful, her mind a whirlwind of emotions.

They disappeared through the palace gates, each of them harboring their own secrets and desires, their paths intertwined, their destinies intertwined in a dance of ambition, betrayal, and love.

CHAPTER FORTY

"The Shadow's Dance"

The Eldoria Palace, a labyrinth of secrets and shadows, hummed with a nocturnal energy. Kai, his heart pounding against his ribs, stood outside Daichi 's chambers, his body tense, his senses alert. He adjusted the mask covering his face, its darkness concealing his features, his true intentions.

He pulled out a slim, wickedly sharp knife, its blade gleaming in the dim light, a weapon he had chosen carefully, a weapon that would ensure his target lived. For a moment, his fingers lingered on the hilt of the sword strapped to his back, a weapon of last resort, a tool of destruction.

No, not yet. He needed Daichi alive, his capture the key to his plan.

Across the hall, hidden in the shadows, Miyu prepared her own attack. She strung her bow, her movements precise and deadly, her fingers deftly manipulating the string, her heart filled with a burning rage. She too wore a mask, hers molded into the fierce visage of a hunting bird, a symbol of her deadly intent.

Both moved with a silent grace, their paths converging on the King's chambers, their destinies intertwined in a deadly dance of ambition and vengeance.

The antechamber, a grand space adorned with intricate carvings and opulent tapestries, was illuminated by the flickering light of torches, casting long shadows that danced on the walls. Daichi , oblivious to the danger lurking in the darkness, entered the antechamber, his back to the intricately carved wooden door leading to his private chambers.

Miyu, perched on the rafters above, watched through the shadows, her eyes focused on Daichi , her bow drawn, her arrow nocked and aimed. The air hummed with tension, the silence punctuated by the steady beating of her heart.

As Daichi reached for the door handle, Miyu drew back her bowstring, her fingers tightening, her muscles straining. The air crackled with anticipation, the silence punctuated by the faint whine of the bowstring.

Suddenly, a glint of metal flashed in the dim light. Before Miyu could release her arrow, Kai, concealed in a shadowy alcove, intercepted it with his knife, his movement a blur of speed and precision.

The arrow clattered harmlessly to the floor, a metallic clang echoing through the stillness of the chamber.

Daichi , startled by the sound, whirled around, his hand instinctively reaching for his sword.

But he saw nothing in the darkness, only shadows dancing on the walls.

Confused, but sensing danger, Daichi quickly disappeared into his private chambers, slamming and bolting the door behind him, his heart pounding with a mixture of fear and a surge of adrenaline.

Miyu, furious at this unexpected interference, leaped from the rafters, her body a blur of motion, her movements fluid and graceful. She landed in a crouch, her bow drawn, her eyes narrowed, her gaze trained on the shadowy figure who dared to defy her.

"I know someone are there," Kai said, his voice a low rumble that echoed through the chamber, his tone laced with a mixture of suspicion and a hint of challenge. "Show yourself!"

Miyu straightened, stepping into a pool of moonlight filtering through a nearby window, her form illuminated by the silvery light.

Kai, his sword now drawn, his body tense, his senses alert, took a step back, surprised by his adversary's grace and agility.

"Who are you?" Miyu asked, her voice low, dangerous, her eyes burning with a fiery intensity that sent a shiver down Kai's spine. "Why do you protect him?"

"The question is, who are you?" Kai countered, his voice steady, his gaze unwavering, his mind racing, trying to decipher her intentions. "And why do you seek to kill a king?"

Silence descended once again, the only sound the steady rasp of their breaths, the silent tension crackling in the air. They circled each other, two predators sizing each other up, their masked faces betraying nothing but deadly intent, their hearts filled with conflicting desires.

The only sound was the scrape of metal on stone as their deadly dance began, their movements a blur of motion, a deadly ballet of attack and parry, their blades clashing in a symphony of steel.

Miyu's arrows flew with deadly accuracy, each one aimed to kill, each one fueled by a righteous rage. But Kai was too fast, too agile. He deflected them with his sword, his movements fluid and graceful, his reflexes honed by years of survival in the wilderness. He used his intelligence and speed to counter her lethal grace, his mind constantly calculating, his body reacting instinctively.

Finally, in a flurry of motion, Kai disarmed Miyu, his sword striking her bow with a resounding clang. He pressed the tip of his sword against her throat, their bodies inches apart, their gazes locked, their breaths mingling in the stillness of the chamber.

"I need him alive," Kai said, his voice a low growl, his body trembling with the exertion of their fight.

"And I will see him dead," Miyu countered, her voice laced with a defiant anger, her eyes burning with a fire that mirrored the flames of her hatred.

"Cross me, and I will stop you," Kai warned, his voice a mixture of threat and a flicker of something akin to respect.

"Try me," Miyu challenged, her voice a whisper of defiance, her gaze unwavering, her spirit unyielding.

For a moment, their gazes locked. The air crackled with an unspoken challenge, their animosity almost tangible, their hearts beating in unison with the rhythm of their conflict.

Suddenly, the distant sound of approaching footsteps filtered through the palace, a rhythmic beat that echoed through the corridors, a warning that their time was running out.

Miyu's head snapped towards the sound, her eyes widening in alarm, her instincts screaming at her to escape. She acted quickly, kicking out at Kai, her foot connecting with his chest, creating just enough space to slip past him.

She disappeared through an open window, her body a blur of motion, her movements fluid and precise, her escape a testament to her agility and determination.

Kai, knowing he'd been outmaneuvered, his heart pounding with a mixture of frustration and a flicker of respect for his adversary, melted into the shadows, disappearing through another passage just as the palace guards rounded the corner.

"Did you see anything?" a guard asked, his voice filled with concern, his eyes scanning the shadowy room, his senses alert.

"Nothing, sir," another guard replied, his voice a nervous whisper, his gaze fixed on the shadows, his mind replaying the echoes of the clash of steel. "Just a draft."

The door burst open, and Daichi strode into the antechamber, his face a mask of fury, his hand reaching for his sword, his eyes scanning the shadows, his senses on high alert.

"What was that commotion?!" he demanded, his voice a roar that echoed through the chamber, his anger palpable. "Someone was here!"

Kai, who had shed his mask and re-entered the room alongside the other guards, kept his head bowed, his true emotions hidden from the king, his heart pounding with a mixture of relief and a touch of fear.

"Find whoever was responsible!" Daichi commanded, his voice laced with a chilling authority. "Alive. I want answers!"

The guards, their faces a mixture of fear and obedience, scurried away, leaving Kai alone with the king. As Daichi turned to re-enter his chambers, he glanced back at Kai, a flicker of suspicion crossing his features, a faint echo of doubt in his mind.

"You," Daichi said, his voice a low rumble, his gaze piercing Kai's facade. "You seem familiar..."

Kai met his gaze, his expression carefully neutral, his heart pounding in his chest, his mind racing, trying to decipher the king's intentions.

Before Daichi could probe further, another guard rushed up, his face a mixture of urgency and concern, distracting the king with reports of the intruder's escape. Daichi , his curiosity piqued but his priorities clear, dismissed Kai with a wave of his hand, his attention focused on the threat to his kingdom.

Kai, his heart pounding with a mixture of relief and a lingering sense of danger, retreated to the alcove he had used earlier, a place of concealment and a reminder of his near escape.

He removed his mask, breathing a sigh of relief, his face betraying a mixture of fatigue and a flicker of fear.

"That was too close," he said to himself, his voice a low murmur, his mind replaying the encounter, the intensity of the fight, the agility of his opponent. "But who was she?"

He ran a hand through his hair, his mind replaying their encounter, her skill, her lethal grace, the fire in her eyes. Whoever she was, she was no ordinary assassin. And for some reason, he couldn't shake the feeling that this was far from over.

CHAPTER FORTY-ONE

"THE NIGHT OF REVELRY"

The grand hall of Solara Palace glittered with a thousand flickering lamps. Exquisite silks adorned the walls, and the air thrummed with intoxicating melodies of celebration. It was the eve of Akira 's wedding, and the palace overflowed with revelry. Daichi , resplendent in gold and jewels, raised his goblet high.

"Let the music begin! Let us celebrate this joyous occasion!" he declared.

A hush fell over the hall as a troupe of dancers entered, their movements fluid and graceful.

At their center was Miyu, her face partially veiled, her body adorned in silks and jewels that shimmered like moonlight on water. She moved with captivating allure, her eyes searching the crowd until they landed on Kai.

Standing apart from the throng of revelers, Kai was mesmerized. He watched as Miyu danced, her every gesture speaking to him, her eyes reflecting the flickering candlelight and something infinitely deeper. The music swelled, echoing the quickening beat of their hearts. Miyu extended her hand in a silent invitation. Hesitation marked Kai's face, torn between duty and yearning. But something in her eyes, a plea masked by a challenge, compelled him forward.

Stepping into the dance, his initial awkwardness melted away. Their bodies moved together in a graceful, unspoken dialogue, lost in a world of their own. Akira watched from her ornate throne, her eyes burning with jealousy.

The music reached a crescendo before softening into a melody of bittersweet longing. The dancers formed a circle around Kai and Miyu, their movements reflecting the unspoken emotions swirling between the two. In a shared glance, a silent promise was made, a connection forged amidst danger and deceit.

Suddenly, the music stopped. Silence descended upon the hall, heavy and absolute. Daichi staggered back, clutching his chest, whispering urgently to a guard.

"The chest... the elixir... it's gone! Someone has stolen it!"

Panic flashed across the guard's face as he barked orders. The festive atmosphere evaporated, replaced by frantic activity as guards scrambled to search for the missing elixir. Daichi turned to his sister, his expression contrite.

"Akira , my love, I am so sorry. I don't know how this could have happened."

Akira 's face was a mask of disappointment and fury as she rose from her throne. "Then find a solution, brother. Find me a husband. Tonight."

Her eyes scanned the hall, settling on Kai with a calculating glint. Daichi followed her gaze, his face brightening. He clapped a hand on Kai's shoulder, pulling him towards his sister.

"An excellent choice! Kai, you are a man of honor, of courage. Surely you would not deny my sister's hand in marriage?"

Kai was stunned, his mind reeling. He glanced at Miyu, who watched the unfolding drama with a mixture of alarm and steely resolve.

"Your Majesty, I..."

Before he could protest, Akira took his hand, her grip surprisingly strong. Her eyes met Miyu's, a silent challenge passing between them.

This was Miyu's chance. As Daichi turned to address the stunned crowd, Miyu melted into the chaos, drawing a small, deadly knife from beneath her robes. With the stealth of a shadow, she slipped behind the distracted king, pressing the blade against his throat.

"One move, and he dies," she threatened.

The guards froze, their swords half drawn. Kai watched in disbelief as the woman who had captivated him now held the king hostage.

It was her... all along, he realized. She was the one who fought with me yesterday. But why?

He rose from his place beside Akira , his hand hovering near his sword hilt, torn between his duty to the king and the inexplicable pull he felt towards Miyu.

"Who are you? What do you want?" Daichi struggled to stay calm.

"Your death would be a good start..." Miyu tightened her grip on the knife, drawing a thin line of blood on Daichi 's throat. Kai knew he had to act quickly, before the situation spiraled out of control.

He took a step forward, but Akira grabbed his arm with surprising strength. "Don't! Let the guards deal with her!"

Kai hesitated, his gaze locked on Miyu's determined figure. In that instant, he realized he could not stand by and watch her die.

Sensing an opportunity, Miyu used Daichi as a human shield, deftly dodging the guards' attempts to subdue her. But the odds were stacked against her. A guard landed a blow, sending her reeling.

Daichi broke free from her grasp, shoving her away with all his might.

As Miyu stumbled, Daichi grabbed a discarded sword from the floor, his eyes blazing with fury. He lunged at her, burying the blade deep in her shoulder.

"No!" Miyu gasped in pain, crumpling to the floor.

Kai watched in horror as the fight drained from her eyes. He wrenched himself free from Akira 's grasp and rushed towards her, but it was too late. The guards surrounded her, their faces grim.

"Take her away! Lock her up! She will pay for this treachery!" Daichi 's voice trembled with rage.

As the guards dragged the injured Miyu away, their eyes met one last time across the crowded hall. Her gaze held a mixture of defiance and something else—a flicker of recognition, of shared purpose, of something akin to hope.Kai's heart pounded with a confusing mix of anger, concern, and a growing sense of admiration. He watched her disappear into the shadows, knowing their paths were now irrevocably entwined.

CHAPTER FORTY-TWO

"A DANCE OF BLADES AND BROKEN HEARTS"

The dungeon air hung heavy with the stench of stale sweat and fear. Miyu sat on the cold stone floor, her bandaged shoulder throbbing in time with her racing pulse. She glared at the iron bars, her spirit unbroken despite her captivity. Her mind churned with plans of escape, each one more desperate than the last.

Suddenly, a cacophony of noise – the clang of metal, a muffled shout, the thud of bodies hitting stone – erupted from the corridor outside her cell. Miyu scrambled to her feet, every muscle tensed, as a figure, shrouded in darkness, appeared at her cell door.

The figure raised a hand, and with a powerful kick, shattered the lock. Miyu tensed, reaching for a makeshift weapon, her eyes struggling to pierce the gloom. The figure stepped forward, moonlight filtering through the bars revealing a familiar silhouette, a haunting echo of the stranger from the marketplace, from the antechamber... from the dance floor. He wore the same mask, obscuring his features, but his eyes... she'd know those eyes anywhere.

Fury flared in Miyu's chest. "You! You think you can mock me? You stand beside your king while I rot in this cell?"

The figure said nothing. He knelt before her, extending a hand. In his palm lay the familiar mask she wore earlier, her bow, and a quiver of arrows.

"What is this game?" Miyu's voice was sharp with suspicion. "Why return my weapons?"

"No games. No time. Wear this. We escape. Now." His voice was muffled by the mask, but the urgency was palpable. He gestured towards the hallway.

Miyu hesitated, suspicion warring with a desperate longing for freedom. She eyed the mask, the bow... the stranger. "And who are you to decide my fate? Reveal yourself!"

The man remained silent, his gaze unwavering. He knew revealing his identity now would be disastrous for them both. He held her gaze for a beat, then nodded towards the dungeon entrance. "Trust me."

His words, spoken with quiet intensity, sparked something in Miyu's chest. It wasn't trust, not entirely, but a flicker of reckless hope. She grabbed the mask, her fingers brushing against his for the briefest of moments, sending an unexpected jolt through her. She pulled the mask over her face, concealing her features. He was right; there was no time for explanations, not now. Survival first, answers later.

Grabbing her bow and arrows, Miyu followed the masked stranger as he melted into the shadows of the corridor. Before stepping out of the cell, she paused, her eyes glinting dangerously. She pulled a burning torch from the wall and tossed it towards a cluster of explosive barrels she'd spotted earlier.

The dungeon erupted in a fiery explosion, buying them precious time as they disappeared into the labyrinthine corridors of the palace.

Bursting through the door, sword raised, he was prepared to fight his way to the king. But the sight that greeted him was not what he expected. Daichi stood in the center of the room, sword drawn, his face a mask of cold fury. But it was Akira who caught Kai off guard. She stood beside her brother, clutching a robe to her chest, her eyes wide with a mixture of terror and... something else... a desperate hope.

"You! You dare show your face here again?" Daichi spat.

Kai started to lower his sword, wanting to explain, to reason with the king. "Daichi , listen to me... I don't want to fight..."

But Daichi wasn't interested in explanations. He lunged, his attack fueled by fury and paranoia. Kai deflected the blow, but Daichi was relentless, his every strike imbued with a cold, calculating rage. The room became a whirlwind of clashing steel, the air thick with the scent of sweat and fear.

Akira watched the fight, her face ashen, her heart torn between the two men who held her fate in their hands. When Kai gained the upper hand, disarming the king momentarily, Akira acted. She lunged for Kai, but instead of attacking, she tore the mask from his face.

"Kai?" Akira 's voice was filled with shock and betrayal.

Daichi froze, his sword clattering to the floor. He stared at Kai, his features contorting in disbelief, in betrayal. "You... it was you all along? You were playing me this entire time?"

"This isn't what it looks like... I can explain..." Kai glanced from Akira to Daichi , his voice urgent.

But Daichi was beyond reason. He grabbed his fallen sword, his face a mask of rage and heartbreak. "You dare betray my trust? My sister's affections? You will pay for this treachery!"

Kai, still reeling from Akira 's revelation and the king's sudden shift, stumbled. He fell to his knees, bracing himself for the killing blow. But the blow never came.

A sharp gasp. The sickening thud of metal piercing flesh. Kai looked up to see Akira standing behind her brother, her hand buried to the wrist in his back, her face a mask of anguish and grim determination. Daichi cried out, a sound of pure agony and betrayal. He stared at Akira , his eyes wide with a betrayal so profound it eclipsed even the pain.

"Forgive me... brother... But I couldn't... I couldn't let you..." Akira 's voice was choked with tears.

Daichi , his back a bloody ruin, let out a roar of pain and fury. He spun around, his free hand lashing out, grabbing Akira by the throat. She cried out again, this time in surprise and fear as his grip tightened.

"You... you dare...?" His voice was a strangled rasp. He threw her back against the wall, his eyes blazing with a murderous rage that chilled Kai to the bone. Akira slid to the floor, clutching her throat, gasping for air.

Daichi stumbled towards her, pulling the dagger from his back with a grunt of pain. Blood stained his tunic a gruesome crimson.

Kai scrambled to his feet, his hand going to his sword hilt. "Stop! Leave her alone!"

But Daichi ignored him, his focus solely on Akira . He raised the dagger, his face a mask of pain and fury.

"You will betray me? Me? You will choose this... this..." He couldn't even bring himself to say Kai's name. He spat on the ground near her face.

Before Kai could intervene, Daichi brought the dagger down, burying it deep in Akira 's chest. She screamed, a high-pitched, desperate sound that tore through Kai's soul.

Akira crumpled to the floor beside her brother, their lifeblood pooling around them, staining the rug a sickening red. He stood over her, his chest heaving, his entire body wracked with pain and betrayal.

"You... you were always... weak... foolish... just like..." Daichi 's voice was a ragged whisper. He swayed, his hand flying to his chest. The adrenaline that had been keeping him upright deserted him, and he collapsed beside Akira , his body wracked with tremors. Akira , her voice barely a whisper, reached out a hand towards him.

"Brother... I..." But Daichi didn't see her. His eyes were fixed on some distant point, his breath coming in ragged gasps. He stared into the abyss, his face a mask of pain and... something else... regret? Remorse? It was impossible to tell. He slumped against the wall, his eyes glazing over. Dead.

Akira looked at Kai, her vision blurring, her hand clutching his discarded mask. "Go...

Kai... Run..." Her voice was barely a whisper.

Kai scrambled to his feet, picking up his mask. He wanted to help Akira , to make sense of the carnage unfolding around them, but he knew he couldn't. He had to escape, for her sake as much as his own. He cast one last glance at the woman he could have loved, the woman who had just sacrificed everything for him, and fled, disappearing into the shadowed hallways of the palace.

Miyu sprinted around the corner, every nerve in her body screaming danger. There, slumped against the cold stone wall, was Akira . A crimson stain bloomed on her chest, a macabre rose claiming its territory.

"Akira ? What happened?" Miyu rushed to her side, panic clawing at her throat. "Where's Daichi ?"

Akira 's eyes fluttered open, a wave of jealousy crashing over her like a rogue wave. This was the woman she'd seen with Kai, the woman who danced with him, who held his attention in a way no one else had. But the fiery resentment was quickly doused by a wave of searing pain and the chilling realization that time was a cruel mistress, rapidly dwindling.

Akira 's inner monologue screamed, a frantic plea: She was Miyu, she must escape the prison. And I must hide the truth, that I killed my brother...

"Gone..." Akira rasped, her voice barely a whisper.

Miyu lurched closer, suspicion twisting her features. "Gone? What do you mean? Did he escape? Did you let him escape?"

Akira leaned further back, her breaths coming in ragged gasps. Blood seeped from her wound, but the physical torment was a mere shadow compared to the icy fear gripping her heart. Her secret had to remain buried, even in death.

"He..." Akira started, her voice fading.

Miyu closed the distance, her hand hovering near the hidden dagger strapped to her thigh.

"What are you trying to say?" Her voice was a low growl, laced with suspicion. "Tell me what happened to your brother!"

Another cough wracked Akira , spraying blood across her lips.

"My brother gone..." she whispered, her voice barely a tremor in the stillness.

Miyu's fury boiled over. The pieces snapped into place, forming a horrifying picture. "That masked guy," she snarled, the name catching in her throat. "He did something to the king... was he working with you? He... he kidnapped the king? He betrayed me... I thought... I thought he would help me..."

Akira watched Miyu closely, fear battling with a strange sense of pity.

"Who are you talking about?" Akira croaked, confusion flickering in her dimming eyes.

"The masked man," Miyu whispered, a desperate plea clinging to the word.

Understanding dawned on Akira 's face, replaced by a cold dread that crawled into her very core.

"No... you... you don't understand..." she tried to say, but the words wouldn't form, trapped in a prison of their own.

Miyu's patience shattered. "Did you see him? Which way did he go?"

Akira looked up at her, her eyes filled with a chilling cocktail of fear and regret.

"He... he went that way..." Her voice failed her once more.

Miyu didn't wait for more. She bolted towards the clash of steel echoing down the hallway, her heart a drum echoing betrayal, her mind a storm brewing vengeance.

Akira watched her go, her vision blurring. A hand weakly reached for the gaping wound in her chest. Tears welled up, mixing with the crimson staining her cheeks.

"What have I done?" she rasped, a broken whisper. "My selfishness... my lies... I've driven them apart..."

"If... if I had another chance..." she choked out, a desperate wish clinging to her final breaths. "I would give anything... to see them happy... together... even if it meant... sacrificing myself..."

Her last breath escaped in a sigh heavy with regret, carrying with it a silent apology and a prayer for a love that would never bloom. The corridor fell silent, the weight of Akira 's final moments settling like a shroud on the cold stone floor.

The grand hall echoed with the clang of steel, a cacophony of violence that painted the night a bloody red. Kai, his back to the shadows where Miyu crouched, fought with the ferocity of a cornered beast. Each desperate parry, each desperate swing of his sword, screamed of a desperate yearning for freedom, a freedom tantalizingly close yet maddeningly out of reach.

Miyu, cloaked in darkness, no longer saw the noble warrior she once knew. In her eyes, he was a usurper, a betrayer who held her king captive. The arrow nocked on her bowstring felt like an extension of her own righteous fury. This was her moment, the culmination of a desperate plan – to avenge her fallen kingdom, her captured king, and her own bruised heart.

Her finger hovered over the release, a hair's breadth away from unleashing her vengeance.

But fate, a cruel jester in this bloody ballet, had other plans.

A flicker of movement, a glint of steel, caught Kai's eye. He whipped around, his heart pounding a frantic rhythm against his ribs. There, concealed in the shadows, stood Miyu, her bow raised, an arrow aimed straight for his chest.

But Kai wasn't the only one who saw the danger. In that split second, a guard charged towards Miyu, his blade raised high, promising a swift and merciless end.

"NO!" Kai's scream ripped through the air, a primal cry of warning and desperation. He flung his own sword with all his might, the polished metal a silver blur against the dark backdrop.

The guard fell with a choked cry, Kai's blade finding its mark. But the momentum of his attack carried him forward, a tragic domino effect set in motion. His own sword, a loyal companion for countless battles, remained embedded in the guard's chest, leaving him unarmed and vulnerable.

Miyu's eyes widened in shock and disbelief. The world seemed to slow down, each agonizing moment stretched into an eternity. Her finger, poised for vengeance, twitched, releasing the arrow on a trajectory it could no longer be called back from.

It flew true, a harbinger of a love story gone terribly wrong. The arrow found its mark, burying itself deep in Kai's chest.

"Miyu!" His anguished cry resonated through the hall, a symphony of despair echoing in the cavernous space.

Miyu stared, her world dissolving into a kaleidoscope of shock and betrayal. The hand that flew to her side, where a searing pain had erupted, confirmed the horrifying truth. Blood, a crimson stain blooming on her gown, mirrored the one blossoming on Kai's chest.

They collapsed simultaneously, puppets whose strings had been severed by fate's cruel hand.

Kai, brought to his knees by the arrow that pierced his heart, fought for breath, his vision blurring with the dawning realization that he was losing her, the woman he loved more than life itself.

Miyu sank to the ground, the cold stone floor stealing the warmth from her body as her lifeblood seeped out. Her trembling hand reached out, her lips forming his name in a silent plea for forgiveness, for understanding.

Kai, fueled by a love that defied the boundaries of death, crawled towards her. The pain in his chest was a mere whisper compared to the agony of watching the light slowly fade from her eyes. He reached her side, their fingers brushing in a fleeting moment of connection, a spark of love amidst the wreckage of their shattered dreams.

Then, his hand went limp. His eyes, once filled with determination and love, lost their focus, the light dimming into oblivion.

The scene, an impartial observer to this tragic ballet, panned upwards, leaving the carnage behind. It soared above the towering walls of the Solara Palace, focusing on a single window where flames flickered like malevolent spirits.

A deafening roar shattered the night. The earth trembled as the palace erupted in a fiery inferno. Walls crumbled, towers toppled, and the sky filled with a shower of sparks and debris. The inferno, ignited by Miyu's defiant arrow, consumed everything in its path, a pyre for the love story that burned brightly then died a tragic death within its walls.

The final image faded to black, a stark reminder of the destruction wrought by vengeance and the enduring power of love, even in the face of its own demise.

CHAPTER FORTY-THREE

"New Beginnings"

The palace hall was shrouded in an eerie, ethereal glow. Smoke hung in the air, mingling with the ghosts of memories. But something was different tonight. Instead of the mortal forms of Kai and Miyu, two shimmering, translucent figures stood in the flickering light—their spirits, echoes of their former selves, drawn back to a pivotal moment in their shared history.

Kai turned, his ethereal hand instinctively reaching for the sword that was no longer at his side. His spectral gaze locked with Miyu, who stood poised with an arrow of spectral light nocked in her bow. For a heartbeat, the weight of their past lives and mistakes hung between them. Then, with a gasp, Miyu spun away, her arrow finding its mark in the chest of a shadowy soldier who materialized behind her—an echo of the guard who had almost taken her life.

The soldier-spirit cried out, dissolving into motes of light. Miyu stared at her hands, bewildered.

What is happening? Miyu wondered, her thoughts a jumble of confusion. Is this... my past life?

Kai was equally bewildered. Am I dreaming? How did we get here, from our lives to this?

Drawn together by an invisible force, they took tentative steps toward each other. Kai reached out, his hand ghosting over Miyu's cheek. She didn't flinch. He gently removed her mask, his touch a whisper of warmth against her spectral skin. Miyu's eyes widened as she truly saw him—not as the masked stranger, but as the man whose soul had been intertwined with hers for a thousand lifetimes. She reached up and removed his mask, her fingers trembling.

"Kai?" Her voice was a whisper, eyes filling with tears.

"Miyu? Is it really you?"

He nodded, his spectral heart overflowing with a love that transcended time and death. They fell into each other's arms, an embrace more real than anything they'd ever experienced.

"I don't understand," Kai said. "But it feels like a miracle."

Miyu pulled back, searching his eyes. "The gods... they must have done this. They gave us a second chance."

"Why? Why bring us back here? To this moment?"

Miyu looked around at the burning palace. "Maybe this is a lesson. A chance to learn from our past mistakes. To choose differently."

"But how? We were them. We made those choices. We loved and lost... just like this."

Miyu took his hand, her spectral fingers intertwining with his. "Maybe this time, we find a different path. A way to break the cycle."

A deafening crack echoed through the hall as a chunk of the burning ceiling collapsed, showering the ground with sparks.

"We can ponder the mysteries of fate later," Miyu said. "For now, we need to leave. This palace is about to become our tomb... again."

Kai smiled, a glimmer of his old mischievousness returning. "Lead the way, my love."

Together, they raced through the burning palace, their spectral forms gliding over crumbling stone and fallen timbers. They reached the stables just as the entire structure began to collapse. Mounting two spectral horses, they rode away from the inferno as the palace of Solara crumbled into dust and legend.

The spectral riders emerged from the forest, their forms shimmering under the light of the full moon. Behind them, the sky blazed with an eerie orange glow—the funeral pyre of Solara. Miyu reined in her horse, gazing back at the burning city before turning to Kai, her expression a mix of relief and uncertainty.

"We're free," she said softly. "But what do we do now? Where do we go?"

Kai dismounted his horse, extending a hand to help her down. "We'll figure it out.Together."

He saw the worry etched on her face, the uncertainty clouding her eyes. "Hey... it's alright.

We're safe now. Daichi is gone."

"But your task... your grandfather... you were supposed to bring him back alive. How will you claim your birthright now?"

Kai smiled, genuine and heartfelt. "Our path has taken an unexpected turn. Maybe this is for the best."

He saw the doubt linger in her eyes. "Come... let's go to your kingdom."

Miyu raised an eyebrow, surprised. "My kingdom? What for?"

Kai turned his horse, mounting it with agility. "It's time we paid your ministers a visit. I have a feeling they have a throne waiting for their queen."

He nudged his horse into a gallop, heading down the moonlit path towards Lunaria. Miyu hesitated, then kicked her horse into a gallop, following Kai into the unknown.

The streets of Lunaria were dark and quiet, the city scarred by war but thrumming with a quiet energy. As they approached the palace, Miyu's hand instinctively reached out, her spectral fingers brushing against Kai's.

"Ready?"

Kai smiled, warmth spreading through his spectral chest. "Let's do this. Together."

They dismounted, their forms shimmering like moonlight on water as they entered the palace gates. The throne room was deserted, the flickering torches casting long, eerie shadows. The ministers rose as one when Miyu entered, their eyes widening at the spectral aura surrounding her.

"Miyu! You've returned!" one minister exclaimed. "We heard the news... Solara... Daichi ... is it true? Did you fulfill your task?"

Miyu hesitated, her gaze flickering towards Kai, who stood silently beside her. She opened her mouth to speak, but no words came out. She turned and walked away, shoulders slumping under the weight of their shared secret.

"Princess? What is the meaning of this?" another minister asked, confused.

Kai stepped forward, his expression unreadable. "She is weary from her journey. We will speak more in the morning."

The ministers exchanged uneasy glances, but before they could protest, Kai guided Miyu towards her chambers, leaving them alone in the echoing silence of the throne room.

CHAPTER FORTY-FOUR

"Coronation"

Sunlight streamed through the window, painting the room in a soft, golden light. Miyu stirred beneath the silken covers, disoriented. A maid entered, her arms laden with silks and jewels.

"My Queen! You must hurry! The people... the ministers... they await your presence!"

Miyu sat up, confused. "Queen? What are you..."

The maid smiled, helping Miyu out of bed. "Your coronation, of course! It is a glorious day for Lunaria!"

Miyu could only stare in bewilderment as the maid helped her into an elaborate gown fit for a queen.

The throne room buzzed with activity. Tapestries adorned the walls, fresh flowers filled the air with their sweet fragrance, and anticipation thrummed in the room. Miyu entered, her head held high, her steps measured and regal. She stopped before the throne, gazing over the assembled court. The ministers bowed low, their faces a mixture of respect and awe.

"The people are waiting, Your Majesty. They are eager to see their new queen," a minister said.

Miyu followed the minister onto the balcony overlooking the city square. A roar erupted from the crowd below. People cheered, their voices echoing through the streets of Lunaria. Miyu looked out at the sea of faces, her heart sinking.

"I... I can't do this. I must address them. Tell them the truth. I... I failed in my task. Daichi ... he is dead. But I did not defeat him."

The ministers gasped, their faces paling. "Queen Miyu... what are you saying? Such words could throw the kingdom into chaos!" one minister said, his voice hushed with concern.

Miyu's shoulders slumped. "But I cannot lie to them. I cannot accept this crown under false pretenses."

She turned back towards the balcony, but Kai stepped forward, his presence a calming force.

"My Queen speaks the truth. She did not defeat Daichi ," he said clearly.

A stunned silence descended upon the court. Miyu turned to Kai, eyes wide with surprise and confusion.

"Daichi is dead. Solara will not rise again. This I swear," Kai continued.

The ministers exchanged uncertain glances, but Kai's calm assurance soothed their fears.

"We believe you, Kai. But... how did this happen?" a minister asked.

Kai explained what transpired in Daichi 's chambers—Akira 's desperate act, the king's death, their spectral escape. He didn't reveal their true natures, but painted a picture of Miyu's courage, of her unwavering resolve to free her people from tyranny.

When he finished, the ministers stared at Miyu with newfound respect and admiration.

"Forgive us, Your Majesty. We misjudged you. You have proven yourself to be a worthy ruler, a true heir to your father's legacy," one minister said, bowing low.

He stepped forward, bearing a magnificent crown crafted from gold and precious gems—the crown of the Queen of Lunaria. But Miyu raised a hand, stopping him.

"No. This is not my destiny."

She turned to Kai, her eyes shining with a love that transcended lifetimes.

"He is the true hero of this tale. He is the one who deserves to wear this crown."

The court fell silent, their gazes shifting from Miyu to Kai, their faces etched with confusion.

Kai stared at Miyu, his heart overflowing with love and gratitude. He'd thought he'd lost everything when he chose to save her life, but now he realized he'd gained more than he could ever have dreamed.

"If the court agrees, I will humbly accept this honor," Kai said, his voice steady.

The ministers conferred briefly, then nodded their assent.

"Very well," one minister said. "We will hold a new coronation. Kai, the hero of Solara, shall be crowned King of Lunaria."

The cheers of the crowd echoed through the palace, a triumphant sound that heralded a new era for Lunaria. As Kai stood before his people, Miyu at his side, he knew that their journey was far from over. They had been given a second chance—not just to live, but to love, to rule, and to build a future together.

In their hearts, they carried the memories of their past lives, the lessons of their shared history. And with each step they took, they forged a new destiny—one filled with hope, with promise, and with the unbreakable bond of their eternal love.

Years passed, and under the reign of King Kai and Queen Miyu, Lunaria flourished. The kingdom blossomed into a beacon of peace and prosperity. Their love story became legend, a tale of courage and sacrifice, of redemption and second chances.

They ruled wisely, guided by the lessons of their past and the strength of their bond. They built a future filled with hope and promise, their hearts forever entwined.

As they stood together, watching the sun set over their kingdom, they knew that they had truly broken the cycle. They had found their way back to each other, across lifetimes and realms, and in doing so, they had forged a new destiny—one where they could live, love, and rule together, for all eternity.

CHAPTER FORTY-FIVE

"The Tapestry of Fate"

The cosmic realm shimmered like a breathtaking tapestry woven from stardust and dreams. The Elder God, a being of pure energy and infinite wisdom, watched as the final scene unfolded.

Kai and Miyu, bathed in ethereal light, clasped hands and gazed upon the reincarnated souls of their future selves. Behind the Elder God, his Assistant shifted nervously, brow furrowed with confusion.

"Great One... What just transpired?" the Assistant asked, his voice tinged with uncertainty.

"Was this all... orchestrated?"

The Elder God turned, a gentle smile gracing his ageless features. "Yes, my child. It was all part of my design. A cosmic play, crafted to teach these souls a valuable lesson."

"But why create such a convoluted path for V and Ria? Their lives... their struggles... were they merely a reflection of Kai and Miyu's ancient trials?" the Assistant inquired, his confusion deepening.

The Elder God chuckled, a sound like a thousand wind chimes echoing through the void.

"Every soul carries within it the echoes of its past lives, my child. The challenges, the triumphs, the loves, and the losses – they shape us, mold us, even across millennia. Their masks became their curse after they died."

"But why send Kai and Miyu back as spirits? To observe their own failings reflected in these new lives?" the Assistant pressed on, seeking clarity.

"Precisely! They needed to understand the depths of their connection, to see how their choices, their fears, had reverberated through lifetimes," the Elder God explained, his voice patient.

The Assistant whispered, "Your ways are truly inscrutable, Great One. At first, I feared... I feared I had erred, that the threads of fate had become tangled."

The Elder God's smile widened. "Fear not, little one. Your misstep simply added a bit of... spice to the narrative."

The Elder God's voice then boomed, echoing through the cosmic realm. "Listen, child.

Through this journey, Kai and Miyu have learned the weight of their mistakes. I have shown them the trials they faced, the solutions they overlooked... all through the lives of V and Ria."

The Assistant bowed low, cheeks flushing with a mixture of relief and embarrassment.

"Kai and Miyu could not find balance. Love and ambition warred within them, their trust shattered. They clung tightly to their own desires, unwilling to sacrifice. But V and Ria... they embraced sacrifice. They lifted each other, weaving love and purpose into a harmonious whole. They were ready to lay down their lives, one for the other," the Elder God continued, his voice softer but with a hint of steel. "That is why I orchestrated this game of fate. To show Kai and Miyu the path they'd strayed from, and grant them a second chance... when they finally understood the depths of their failings."

"But Great One... Kai and Miyu... their souls have found peace, their love rekindled. But what of V and Ria? Their struggles... were they all for naught?" the Assistant asked, his voice heavy with concern.

The Elder God turned back towards the vision of Earth, a knowing smirk playing on his lips.

"Every ending is but a new beginning, my child. The tapestry of fate is ever-weaving, and even the smallest threads can create the most magnificent patterns. V and Ria, in their own way, taught Kai and Miyu the true meaning of love, of sacrifice, of unwavering support."

The Assistant watched the Elder God with wide eyes, absorbing the profound truth.

"Kai learned to understand Miyu's strength by witnessing V and's dedication, and Miyu learned the depth of Kai's love by seeing Ria's unwavering faith. Their struggles were not in vain, for they served a greater purpose – to heal the wounds of lifetimes and bind these souls together for eternity," the Elder God concluded, his voice filled with a serene certainty.

The cosmic realm continued to shimmer, a testament to the eternal dance of fate and the boundless wisdom of the Elder God. And as Kai and Miyu stood together, their spirits intertwined in a love that transcended time and space, they knew that their journey had only just begun.

CHAPTER FORTY-SIX

"A New Life"

Rain lashed against the windows, blurring the cityscape outside. V, dressed in a crisp white shirt and tie, jolted upright at his desk, a gasp escaping his lips. He stared at the unfamiliar files spread out before him, his mind a whirlwind of confusion and a lingering sense of wrongness.

"What...? Where...?" he whispered, scrambling to his feet and knocking over a cup of now-cold tea. The scent of jasmine filled the air, a strangely comforting aroma amidst the disorientation.

He looked around the spartan office – framed degrees on the wall, a bookshelf overflowing with law books, a nameplate on the desk that read "V, Govt Officer."

"What am I doing here? The last thing I remember... the street... the rain..." V's voice rose in panic as he glanced down at his clothes, his hands trembling as he touched the expensive fabric of his shirt. "This isn't... I wasn't..."

The door opened, and his Personal Assistant, a kind-faced man in his late forties, hurried in.

"Sir! Are you alright? I heard a noise..." The Assistant noticed V's panicked state, his brow furrowing with concern. "Sir, you look pale. Should I call a doctor?"

"No... no doctor... I just... This office... this... life... it's not The door swung open again, revealing a little girl about five years old, her bright eyes sparkling with mischief. She clutched a drawing, the colors running slightly from the rain that clung to her raincoat.

"Daddy!" she called out, rushing towards him and throwing her small arms around his legs.

He stared down at her, his mind reeling, his heart pounding against his ribs.

"Daddy...?" he whispered, kneeling down, his hands hovering over her shoulders as if afraid to touch, to break this strange, impossible reality.

The little girl beamed up at him, her smile as bright as the sun he could barely remember.

"Happy birthday, Daddy! Happy anniversary!" She held up the drawing, a riot of color depicting a man, a woman, a little girl, and a little boy, all holding hands beneath a bright yellow sun. "Mommy helped me make it!"

V's breath caught in his throat. He looked from the drawing to his daughter, his mind desperately trying to bridge the gap between this life, this reality, and the fragmented memories of another life that ended in a cold, rainy street.

Before he could speak, his daughter grabbed his hand, tugging him towards the door. "Come on, Daddy! Let's go home! Mommy's waiting!"

He let her pull him along, his mind spinning. He glanced back at his Assistant, who smiled reassuringly.

"Don't worry, sir. Go home to your family. I'll take care of everything here."

The car pulled away from the curb, the rhythmic swish of the windshield wipers a soothing counterpoint to the storm raging inside V. He looked at his daughter in the back seat, her head bent over a book, her brow furrowed in concentration. She looked up and caught his eye, her face breaking into a smile that would melt the coldest heart.

He smiled back, a genuine smile this time, a flicker of something warm and true igniting in the depths of his being. He didn't understand how he got here, to this life, this family, but as he watched his daughter's laughter fill the car, he couldn't escape the feeling that somehow... someway... he was exactly where he was supposed to be.

CHAPTER FORTY-SEVEN

"Echoes of the Past"

Rain drummed a steady rhythm against the roof of the archery range. Ria, dressed in a simple but elegant dress, jolted awake at her desk, a wave of disorientation washing over her. She stared at the familiar target boards and the rows of bows and arrows lining the wall. A strange sense of déjà vu tugged at the edges of her mind.

"Mommy! Wake up! We have to go to the park! I left Mr. Snuggles there this morning, and it's starting to get dark!" Her son's high-pitched, insistent voice cut through the rhythmic drumming of the rain.

Ria stared down at her little boy, about four years old, her heart pounding in her chest. His voice washed over her like a warm wave, chasing away the lingering chill of a dream she couldn't quite remember. But why did it feel like she was hearing him for the first time?

How can I understand him? What's happening? she wondered, her thoughts a whirlpool of confusion.

"Come on, Mommy! Please! Mr. Snuggles will be scared all alone in the rain!" Her son tugged at her dress, his small hand pulling her towards the door.

Ria let her son guide her, her mind spinning. As she passed by a mirror hanging on the wall, her reflection stopped her in her tracks. She was wearing a soft pink dress that complemented her complexion, the fabric draped gracefully around her slender frame. A Wedding Ring , a symbol of marriage, rested against her skin, its weight surprisingly comforting.

Her gaze traveled to the wall behind her, drawn to a collection of medals and framed photographs – images of her, younger and full of fire, holding a bow and arrow with a triumphant smile on her face. Local competitions... National championships... World Archery Federation...

What...? These medals... this life... it's all... Is this a dream? But I can hear him... feel him... Her mind battled with the impossible as she looked at the life laid out before her.

"Mommy, come on! We need to get Mr. Snuggles and go home. Don't you remember? It's your anniversary! And Daddy's birthday!" Her son's voice pulled her back to the present.

Anniversary? Birthday? A cold dread washed over her, a terrifying sense of displacement.

Anniversary? Birthday? What is he talking about? Who... who is his father?

Her son, oblivious to her internal turmoil, continued to tug at her hand, his excitement bubbling over. Ria hesitated for a moment longer, her mind grappling with the impossibility of her situation, before allowing her son to lead her out into the rain-swept street. She grabbed an umbrella, a strange sense of peace washing over her, as if a missing piece had slotted into place within her soul.

She still didn't understand, but as she followed her son's excited chatter, she couldn't shake the feeling that she was exactly where she was supposed to be. The rain fell steadily around them, but in the warmth of her son's hand and the familiarity of the path they walked, Ria found a sense of belonging. Her questions lingered, but for now, the love and urgency in her son's voice guided her forward.

CHAPTER FORTY-EIGHT

"THE REUNION"

Raindrops fell in a steady rhythm, creating a shimmering curtain across the park. Ria's son dashed from bush to bush, his little raincoat a bright splash of color against the gray backdrop. He was on a mission to find Mr. Snuggles, his voice echoing through the park as he called out the plush toy's name.

Ria watched him, her brow furrowed with a mixture of concern and a lingering sense of disorientation. She held the umbrella over her head, the rain pattering against the fabric like a thousand tiny drums.

How can I understand him? What's happening? she wondered, trying to piece together the fragmented memories that swirled in her mind. The park seemed both familiar and strange, the rain-soaked paths pulling at her heart with an inexplicable sense of nostalgia.

Meanwhile, in a car parked nearby, V's daughter pressed her nose against the window, her eyes wide with excitement. "Daddy, look! It's Mommy! And Yuki! They're at the park! Stop the car! Stop the car!"

V's heart leapt into his throat as he followed his daughter's gaze. His eyes widened as he spotted Ria and her son in the distance. Ria? Could it really be her?

Before he could fully process the sight, his daughter threw open the car door and dashed out into the rain. "Wait! You'll catch a cold!" V grabbed the umbrella from the passenger seat and raced after his daughter, calling out her name.

Ria's son spotted his sister racing towards them, his face lighting up. "Mommy! Look! It's Yuna! And Daddy's here too!" He ran towards his sister, his excitement palpable.

Ria slowly turned, her eyes widening as she saw V running towards them. The rain plastered his hair to his forehead, his white shirt clinging to his broad shoulders. For a heartbeat, time seemed to stop.

All she could see was him – his familiar features, the concern in his eyes, the way his smile always crinkled the corners of his eyes. V... it's really him.

She lifted the umbrella, shielding him from the downpour as he came to a stop before her.

"Ria...? What... what are you...?" His voice was a mix of disbelief and cautious hope. He stared at her, his gaze drawn to the dress she was wearing, to the wedding ring glinting against her skin. A thousand unspoken questions swirled in his eyes.

A joy she didn't quite understand bubbled up inside Ria, washing away all the confusion and fear. She dropped the umbrella, letting the rain wash over her as she rushed into his arms, burying her face in his chest. He hesitated for a heartbeat, stunned by the suddenness of her embrace, then wrapped his arms around her, holding her tight as if afraid she'd disappear. The warmth of her body against his, the familiar scent of her hair, the rapid beat of her heart against his chest – it was all so real, so achingly familiar, that it sent a tremor through his soul.

As they stood there, locked in an embrace that defied the rain and the confusion swirling around them, Ria remembered. It's his birthday. Her anniversary. Their anniversary.

She pulled back slightly, her eyes shining with tears and a love that transcended lifetimes.

"Happy birthday, V. I love you," she whispered, her voice trembling with emotion. "These words... they mean everything to me."

His name on her lips... He had never heard it sound so beautiful. She leaned forward,pressing a kiss to his forehead, a kiss filled with all the love and longing that words could never express.

V closed his eyes, the world shrinking down to the feel of her lips against his skin, the rain washing over them like a blessing, the echo of laughter from their children filling the air. He understood. He pulled her close again, burying his face in her hair, holding her as if he'd never let go.

As if guided by an unseen hand, the rain stopped. The clouds parted, revealing a sky washed clean, a sunbeam breaking through the gray, painting the park in a soft, golden light. A gentle breeze stirred the leaves in the trees, showering them with a confetti of brightly colored petals.

Their son, clutching Mr. Snuggles tightly in his arms, ran up to them, his face beaming. His sister followed close behind, giggling. V and Ria knelt down, their arms opening wide as their children rushed into their embrace. They laughed, the sound joyous and unrestrained, a symphony of love and gratitude.

They were a family. Whole and complete. As they piled into the car, heading home to a life filled with love, laughter, and the promise of new beginnings, V caught Ria's eye. Their gazes met, a silent understanding passing between them. They were home, finally home, and they would never let go again.

CHAPTER FORTY-NINE

"THE RETURN"

The front door burst open, and V and Ria's children raced into the house, their laughter echoing through the hallway. Close behind them, V and Ria entered, their faces still flushed from the rain and the overwhelming joy of their reunion.

Ria froze, her eyes widening in disbelief. Sitting in the living room, sipping tea and chatting, were her parents, their faces etched with the familiar lines of love and laughter that she thought she'd never see again. Tears welled up in her eyes, and she rushed towards them, her heart pounding in her chest.

"Mom! Dad!" she cried, throwing her arms around them, hugging them both tightly, the tears flowing freely now.

Her parents were startled by her sudden outburst, their faces filled with concern. "Ria, my darling, what's wrong? What happened? You just left this morning!"

Ria pulled back, her eyes shining with a joy so profound it bordered on disbelief. "Nothing's wrong... everything's... everything's perfect." She hugged them again, holding on as if they might disappear.

V watched the scene unfold, a lump forming in his throat. Her parents... they're... alive? He turned and rushed towards the room that used to belong to his own parents.

He found his father sitting in an armchair, reading a newspaper. V hesitated for a moment, his heart pounding, then walked towards his father, his steps slow and uncertain. "Dad..."

His father looked up, a smile spreading across his face. "V? What are you doing home so early? And look at you, soaked to the bone!"

V knelt beside his father, his arms wrapping around him in a hug that conveyed a lifetime of unspoken love and gratitude. "Dad... where's Mom?"

His father chuckled. "She's in her room, fussing over some new fabric for a dress. You know how she is."

V released his father and rushed towards his mother's room, his heart pounding with a hope that felt both terrifying and exhilarating.

He paused at the doorway, his breath catching in his throat. His mother, Sylvie, stood by the window, her back to him, carefully folding a bolt of vibrant silk. The sunlight filtering through the sheer curtains illuminated her silvering hair, casting a halo around her.

He remembered the coldness of her skin in the morgue, the empty ache in his heart as he watched her lowered into the ground. But now... now she was here, alive and vibrant, a living testament to the impossible.

Tears streamed down his face as he walked towards her, his steps slow and reverent.

"Mom...?"

Sylvie turned, her face breaking into a warm smile. "V? What a surprise! Why are you home so early? And look at you, drenched from the rain!" She pulled him towards the bed, her hands gently brushing the wet hair from his forehead.

He leaned into her touch, the warmth of her hand a balm to his soul. He wrapped his arms around her, burying his face in her shoulder, his body shaking with sobs he could no longer hold back.

Sylvie held him close, her hand stroking his hair, her heart filled with a love that transcended understanding.

Later, in their bedroom, V and Ria sat on their bed, surrounded by photographs spread out across the covers. They traced the outlines of their shared lives with their fingers, their hearts overflowing with gratitude and wonder. Graduation photos captured their youthful dreams and aspirations. Pictures from their wedding day showed their faces beaming with joy and the promise of forever. Snapshots from their honeymoon – Ria and V cuddling a baby panda in China, V and Ria beaming as he fed a baby elephant in India. Pictures of their children, their smiles a reflection of their own happiness. Family photos captured the love that bound them all together.

It was a tapestry woven from the threads of a life they almost lost, a life that had been returned to them, richer and more beautiful than they could have ever imagined. Ria leaned against V's shoulder, her eyes sparkling with happiness.

"We have everything we ever wanted, V. A second chance, a life filled with love... It's like a dream come true."

V kissed her forehead. "More than a dream, Ria. A miracle." He paused, his expression turning thoughtful. "And we owe it all... to them."

Ria nodded, her eyes filled with gratitude. "To those spirits... they showed us the way."

"And to Akira ... she sacrificed everything so that we could have this life."

They sat in silence for a moment, their hearts filled with gratitude for the spirits who guided them, for the love that defied time and death, for the second chance they never thought they'd have.

CHAPTER FIFTY

"The Cosmic Realm"

The Assistant floated in the vast expanse of the cosmic realm, exhaustion etched into every line of their ethereal form. Relief coursed through them as they gazed upon the Elder God, who watched with a knowing smile.

"It's finally over," the Assistant murmured, but a flicker of unease crossed their face. "But Aira... her suffering... why?"

The Elder God's eyes softened with ancient wisdom. "Love, my child. Aira sacrificed for love and friendship. She understood that V and Ria needed to learn its true power, even through pain. I merely guided them to the destinies they deserved. And I gave Aira a second chance to correct the mistake she made."

The Assistant shook their head, still troubled. "All that suffering... was it truly necessary?"

A gentle chuckle echoed through the realm. "I didn't give them the life they wanted. I gave them the life they needed and deserved."

The Assistant's brows knitted together, a new question forming. "Great One, I'm puzzled. If Kai and Miyu find happiness and avoid their tragic fate, wouldn't that prevent the reincarnations of V and Ria? How can they be reborn if their past lives don't end as they should?"

The Elder God's smile grew, a knowing glint in his eyes. "Ah, a keen observation, Assistant.

You touch upon the very fabric of time and destiny. Kai and Miyu's happiness is but a ripple in the grand tapestry. While their souls are entwined with V and Ria, each life holds its own unique essence. I have separated their fates, granting V and Ria a new destiny, a chance to experience the joy that eluded their past selves."

The Assistant relaxed slightly, a glimmer of hope sparking in their heart. "Finally, some rest."

The Elder God's grin turned predatory. "Rest? Countless souls still await. We're just getting started. Shall we play a new game?"

Horror dawned in the Assistant's eyes as they stared at the Elder God, their form collapsing to the ground. The Elder God watched, their smile widening with malevolent delight.

In the cosmic realm, the Assistant floated, their spirit weary yet relieved after the monumental task. The Elder God observed them with a knowing, serene smile. "It's finally over," the Assistant murmured, but unease lingered. "But Aira... her suffering... why?"

"Love, my child," the Elder God replied. "Aira sacrificed for love and friendship. She knew V and Ria needed to learn the true power of love, even through pain. I merely guided them to the destinies they deserved and gave Aira a second chance to correct her past mistakes."

The Assistant shook their head, still troubled. "All that suffering... was it truly necessary?"

The Elder God chuckled softly. "I didn't give them the life they wanted. I gave them the life they needed and deserved."

The Assistant, still puzzled, asked, "Great One, if Kai and Miyu find happiness and avoid their tragic fate, wouldn't that prevent the reincarnations of V and Ria? How can they be reborn if their past lives don't end as they should?"

The Elder God's smile grew, eyes twinkling with ancient wisdom. "Ah, a keen observation.

Kai and Miyu's happiness is but a ripple in the grand tapestry. While their souls are entwined with V and Ria, each life holds its unique essence. I have separated their fates, granting V and Ria a new destiny, a chance to experience the joy that eluded their past selves."

A glimmer of hope flickered in the Assistant's heart. "Finally, some rest."

The Elder God's grin turned predatory. "Rest? Countless souls still await. We're just getting started. Shall we play a new game?"

Horror dawned in the Assistant's eyes as they collapsed to the ground, the Elder God's smile widening with malevolent delight.

- - - THE END - - -